Murder Of A Werewolf

APRIL FERNSBY

Chapter 1

Gran peered closer at me across her kitchen table and said, "Cassia, this can't go on."

I shifted in my seat. "What can't go on?"

"You know full well. You can't carry on working so hard. You look as if you're getting ready to knock on Death's door. When did you last have a good night's sleep? You've got bags under your eyes. And bags underneath those bags."

I sat back on my chair and tried to defend myself. "We're extremely busy at work. I've got the staff appraisals to do. They won't do themselves."

A twinkle came into Gran's eyes, and she said, "They could. But we'll talk about that another time. Cassia, I'm not nagging you. I'm worried about you."

"There's nothing to worry about. I'm a grown woman. I can take perfectly good care of myself."

I felt a familiar ache at the back of my throat, and before I could stop it, my mouth opened in a huge yawn. I tried my best to curtail it, but it was one of those yawns that takes on a life of its own. As soon as the yawn had done its worst, I snapped my mouth shut and ignored the satisfied look in Gran's eyes.

She wagged a finger at me. "You can't kid me, young lady. You might be twenty-nine years old, but you're still a little girl to me. I know when you're lying to me. I'll make us a fresh cup of tea, and then you can tell me the truth. I want to know what's going on in your life, and," Gran gave me a particularly piercing stare, "I want to know why you've been paying visits to the doctor."

I swallowed. "What? The doctor? How do you know about that?"

Gran heaved herself to her feet. "They still have my number as your contact number. Someone from the surgery phoned me yesterday to let me know you've got a prescription ready at the chemist."

"Oh. Right." I'd forgotten to let the doctor's surgery know about my change of address and telephone number. I'd moved out of Gran's house over a year ago, but I still hadn't got around to letting everyone know. I meant to. But I kept forgetting.

As if reading my thoughts, Gran said, "Don't you want to let all the relevant authorities know you're living on your own now? You don't have to, you know. You're always welcome to come back here anytime. I've left your bedroom just as it is. And there's plenty of room in this old cottage." She smiled at me before turning away and heading towards the kettle.

I felt my face scrunching up. Of course I didn't want to come back here and live with Gran. What sort of a sensible grown-up woman with a respectable job wants to live with her gran? Not me. I've got my own place and a good paying job. I'm far too old to be living with my grandma.

Gran whistled as she filled the kettle and I looked around the cosy kitchen. I couldn't help but smile as my eyes alighted on all the knick-knacks that Gran had collected over the years. She liked to collect a souvenir of every place she'd ever visited, no matter how tacky the souvenir was. When I was old enough, she let me pick the souvenirs. Being a child, I went for anything big, shiny and gaudy. I smiled more as my glance went to the vivid red telephone box covered in sequins. I had insisted on Gran buying it when we went to London. It stood proudly on one of the kitchen shelves.

I was so lost in my thoughts that I jumped when Gran came back to the kitchen table. She pushed a cup towards me and said, "Drink that. I've made it extra strong. It'll put hairs on your chest."

"I don't want hairs on my chest." I pulled the cup towards me and took a sip. I sighed happily. "I know I've said this before, but you make the best tea, Gran. What do you put in it?"

Gran sat down and tapped the side of her nose. "I put magic in it. Enough about tea. Let's get back to you. Tell me about your work."

I cradled my hands around the cup. "Work is busy. Like I said, I've got staff appraisals coming up and – "

"Yes," Gran interrupted. "They sound immensely boring. Do you enjoy your job?"

I took another drink of the delicious tea before replying, "It's alright. It's a job. It's got good prospects. And a good salary with an excellent pension scheme. And many employee benefits." I abruptly stopped. I sounded like a job advert.

"Hmm. What about that boyfriend of yours? Alex? Andrew? Adam? Whatever his name is."

"Alastair. Gran, you know his name. You've met him twice."

"Have I? He can't have made much of an impression on me." Gran's mouth twitched, and she quickly took a drink of tea.

I held in my sigh. Gran had never taken to Alastair. Not many people did.

"Alastair is helping me with the staff appraisals. He's got much more experience than me. He doesn't want me to get it wrong. He wants me to impress the managers. If I'm lucky, I could get a promotion within the next twenty-four months."

"I see. That's enough about your work. The lady on the phone yesterday told me the doctor's prescribed strong sleeping tablets for you. Why aren't you sleeping? Are you worrying about something? You always were a worrier. And why have you got ulcer tablets in your handbag? You're too young to be getting ulcers. I saw all those painkillers in there too."

I opened my mouth to ask her when she'd looked in my bag. Tears sprang unexpectedly to my eyes, and I burst into tears.

Gran was at my side in a flash. She moved the cup from my hands and put her arms around me. "There, there, Cassia. Let it all out. You go ahead and have a good cry. I don't mind you using my sleeve as a tissue."

I don't know what came over me, but once I started to cry, I just couldn't stop. I didn't know a person could cry for so long. Poor Gran, her sleeve was sopping wet by the time I eventually stopped. She could have wrung it out.

I wiped my wet cheeks and attempted a smile. "Sorry, Gran. I don't know what's wrong with me."

Gran gave me a searching look. In a soft voice, she said, "You do know what's wrong. You've known for a while. You've been hiding your true feelings; you've been trying to dampen them down with work and medications. That never works."

I nodded. Gran was right. I'd been miserable for a long time. Something wasn't right in my life. I felt like I was living the wrong life. And I didn't know how to make things better.

Gran pulled her chair closer and sat back down. She put her hand on top of mine. "Cassia, I should have told you the truth years ago. It was entirely my fault that I didn't. I wanted you to have a normal life and to make your own path in life. But I can see where that has taken you. I can't stand by and let you continue as you are. You're heading towards an early grave, and I won't have that."

"What do you mean by the truth? Gran? You're starting to scare me. Have I got some genetic disease?

Some family problem that's going to cut me off in my prime? Is that why I feel so awful all the time? And why I can't sleep? What's wrong with me?"

Gran squeezed my hand. "There's nothing wrong with you. But you're not living the life you're supposed to. You're not being true to yourself. You're denying who you are."

I tried to look away from Gran's loving gaze. Part of me wanted to end this conversation and run out of the door. I had those staff appraisals to do, and they wouldn't do themselves.

In a voice barely above a whisper, I said, "Gran, what's wrong with me?"

Gran smiled. "There's nothing wrong with you. Cassia Winter, you're a witch. Just like me."

Chapter 2

I pushed my chair back and sprang to my feet. I pointed a shaky finger at Gran's cup and cried out, "What have you put in your tea? Have you been messing about with some funny herbs? I told you not to buy anything off the internet!"

Without waiting for an answer, I stormed over to the kitchen window, planted my hands on my hips and glared out at Gran's garden. I said, "Okay, tell me where the dodgy herbs are, and I'll get rid of them straight away. Or are you growing them somewhere out of view? Have you got a secret polytunnel set up somewhere? Perhaps in the attic? Or down in the – " I stopped short. I nearly said the forbidden word.

I turned accusing eyes on Gran. "Well? What have you got to say about making that ridiculous statement? A witch! Ha! Don't you think I'd know if I were a witch?"

Gran was watching me calmly from her seated position. Her cat, Oliver, was nestled on her knee. His glossy black fur caught the soft light in the room, and I had the overwhelming urge to stroke his soft back. Oliver had always had that effect on me. It was almost like he was … bewitched? No. That's ridiculous.

Gran tickled Oliver behind his ears and then looked at me. She said, "You can rant and rave all you like. It's true. You know it's true, Cassia. And as for growing funny herbs, why would I want to do that? What do you take me for? Some underground drugs baron? A kingpin? Is that what they call it? Do you think I'm secretly selling batches of drugs to my neighbours?" She smiled down at Oliver. "Although, some of the miserable blighters could do with cheering up."

I put my hands behind my back and began to pace the kitchen. "No, I don't think you're a drugs dealer. But why would you say that about us being witches? It's ridiculous. I'd know. Wouldn't I?" I stopped pacing. 'Gran, wouldn't I know if I were a witch?"

Gran gave me a kind look. "You do know. Deep down you know. You've always been different from other people. You can easily pick up on what others are feeling; you're a sensitive soul. Do you still experience that? It used to happen often when you were little. And you used to tell me about it."

I shrugged and returned to my seat. "Everyone can sense the atmosphere in a room or what people are feeling. It's nothing special."

"It is special." Gran looked me straight in the eyes. "Do you still get those feelings?"

I tried to look away from her piercing stare, but it was impossible. "Now and again. I haven't had as many incidents in the last few months."

Gran nodded. "I see. And when did your health problems start? Around the same time?"

I thought about that and then gave Gran a slow nod. "That doesn't mean anything."

Oliver turned his green eyes my way. Was that pity in his eyes? Cheeky cat. I didn't need his pity.

Gran went on, "Cassia, you're suppressing your natural abilities and talents. Your body knows that, and it's rebelling. Deep, deep down you know I'm right. Just think about that for a moment."

Oliver let out a little meow as if agreeing with Gran.

I bowed my head and looked at the table. There was a feeling in the pit of my stomach. It wasn't dread, but it was something I was trying to hide. It was like I knew something was true but I didn't dare admit it to myself for fear of the consequences. I put my hands on my stomach and closed my eyes. I concentrated on the feeling. There was a sudden fluttering as if a tiny butterfly had woken up and was flapping its wings. A tiny warmth shot through my stomach.

I smiled. I didn't know what this feeling was, but it felt wonderful.

I was brought out of my trance by Gran saying, "There it is, Cassia. That's the feeling you're looking for. You're letting the truth in. I can tell by your face that it's only a small feeling, but we can live with that for now. Tell me how Stanley's doing?"

The butterfly in my stomach froze. "Stanley? Why are you asking about him?"

Gran stroked Oliver's back. "Oliver here hasn't seen his brother for a few months. You usually bring him with you when you come for a visit."

This time, Oliver fixed me with an accusatory glance. How could a cat have so many expressions?

"Erm. Stanley's fine. Gran, do you want a fresh cup of tea?" I made to stand up.

"Cassia, stay right where you are. What's wrong with Stanley? Tell us the truth, there's no point lying."

I sighed heavily. Oliver and Stanley have been with Gran for years, and she let me take Stanley with me when I moved out. Oliver and Stanley – yes, Gran is a huge Laurel and Hardy fan. I looked again at Oliver's thick, black fur. Stanley had looked like that when we first moved out. He didn't look like that now.

Gran tapped her hand on the table. "I'm waiting."

Oliver flicked his tail in the air to show he was waiting too.

I looked away from their expectant faces and addressed my comments to the kitchen door. "He's a bit different. I think he's going through a phase."

"Explain yourself. And look at us. There's no point talking to the door. It won't listen."

I put a smile on my face before looking back at Gran and Oliver. "I'm sure it's nothing, but Stanley's been off his food for a while. I took him to the vets, but he couldn't find anything wrong. And his fur has turned a bit grey."

"A bit grey?" Gran arched an eyebrow.

"Well, a lot grey. He's still got bits of black fur, but it's mainly grey." Guilt washed over me as I thought about Stanley. "And he's lost weight. Honestly, Gran, I don't know what's wrong with him. I am worried about him, and I'm trying my best to make him right."

"There's something else, isn't there?"

I hated it when Gran was in my head. She had this annoying ability to know when I was hiding something. A thought shot into my head - it's because she's a witch! I pushed that stupid thought right out.

Oliver let out an impatient howl. He was being a real pain in the rear end today.

I said, "Stanley's been going to funerals."

"Pardon?"

"Funerals. He keeps going to funerals."

"How do you know that?"

"Because the people who are at the funerals keep finding him in the church." I hesitated a moment. "They find him sitting on the coffin. He's got a name tag, so they know he belongs to me. When they find him on the coffin, they try to move him, but Stanley lashes out at them. Which is weird because he's not a violent cat." I saw a hint of a smile on Gran's face. "It's not funny. It's embarrassing. People in funeral attire are constantly turning up at my door with Stanley in their arms. Most of them think it's sweet that an unknown cat would pay their respects to their deceased relative, but a few have been furious and threatened to report me to the police."

Gran shook her head. "He's showing classic symptoms."

"Of what? Being a mad cat?"

"He's not fulfilling his destiny. He's your familiar. All witches have a familiar. Stanley's not doing what he's supposed to be doing, and now he's turned all morbid. He's more interested in the dead than the living."

I was about to disagree with Gran, but then I thought about all the dead mice Stanley kept bringing into the house. He'd lay them in a row on the kitchen floor and stare sadly at them. But morbid? Did cats become morbid?

I gulped. "Gran, is this all my fault? Have I done this to Stanley?"

Gran shook her head. "None of this is your fault. I should have told you the truth earlier. I wanted to protect you. But look where that's got me. You're heading for an early meeting with the Grim Reaper, and your cat is close behind you." She lifted Oliver's furry chin and said to him, "It's time, don't you think so?"

Oliver gave her a slow nod.

Unease settled on me. "Time for what?" I looked at my watch. "Oh? Is that the time. I really must be going."

Gran said, "You're not going anywhere. Not until you know the full truth about yourself. This is a life and death situation. Your life and death." She pushed herself to her feet. She winced in pain.

Alarm bells rang in my head, and I was over to Gran's side in a flash. Gran was never in pain. Never ever. She was always in full health. I'd never even known her to have a cold.

I put my hand on Gran's arm. "Are you alright? Are you in pain?"

"Just a twinge. It's nothing. Stop fussing. Cassia, we're going into the cellar."

The cellar - the forbidden word. My forbidden word, not Gran's.

My hand dropped from Gran's arm. "No."

"We have to."

"No. No!" I turned away from Gran and ran towards the kitchen door. "I'm not going into the cellar, and you can't make me!"

Chapter 3

As I put my hand on the kitchen door handle, a loud hiss sounded out and made me jump. I looked down at where the noise had come from.

Oliver was standing in front of the door, his back arched and his tail standing up as straight as a poker. He hissed at me again.

I took a step back. Oliver had never hissed at me before. He was a gentle, laid back cat. What was going on?

Gran said sharply, "Oliver! Where are your manners? There's no need to talk to Cassia like that."

Talk? Oliver was hissing, not talking. I looked closer at Oliver. He was definitely giving me the evil eye.

Gran carried on talking, "Oliver, step away from the door. If Cassia wants to leave, then let her." She took a sudden, sharp intake of breath.

I spun around and saw Gran leaning heavily on the chair. Her face was creased in pain.

I ran over to her. "Gran! Tell me what's wrong. Do you need the doctor? Let me call Dr Gilbert."

Gran flapped her free hand at me. "It's nothing. It must have been something I ate. I knew I shouldn't have bought that salmon which had been reduced at the supermarket. You should never buy fish that's been reduced." She took her hand off the chair and straightened up. "Cassia, please come into the cellar with me. Just for a few minutes. I want to show you something. It's important. Please?"

Her eyes crinkled up, and she gave me a dimply-cheeked smile. How could I say no to her?

"Okay. Just for a few minutes."

"Super. This way," she said as if I didn't know perfectly well where the dreaded cellar door was.

Gran went down into the cellar first. I'd love to say that it was a dank, dimly-lit room with mould decorating the walls and that there was a disgusting damp smell which seeped into your clothes.

It wasn't like that at all. I wished it was because that would explain my dread of the place. There was no damp smell, no filthy walls, not even a solitary cobweb in evidence. There weren't even any rats in here.

Gran's cellar was lovely. As soon as you stepped into it a smell of fresh air and flowers would float up your nostrils and make its way to your lungs and fill them with joy. Your steps would become lighter as you walked down the pale stone steps and into the spacious, suspiciously light room. There was only one light bulb and no windows in this room, but that bulb was like a mini sun and it filled the cellar with a wonderful light. It was like stepping into a summer's day. Like I said, there were no windows, so where did the smell of fresh air and flowers come from?

It was almost like the cellar was enchanted.

Pah! Ridiculous!

I stomped down the cellar steps and walked over to where Gran was standing.

Gran beamed at me and waved her hand around the room. "I know you don't like this room, but I love it." She nodded her head in the direction of a tall bookcase. "I've got some new books in there if you want to have a look? I've got some great detective ones. I nearly didn't guess who the killer was in some of them!"

I scowled at the bookcase. Who keeps books in a cellar? Any normal cellar would cause the books to rot away with its foul, damp air. But not this cellar. The books were kept as fresh and crisp as the day they'd been printed.

Gran laughed. "Your face will stay that way if you keep scowling. I really don't understand why you hate this room. You used to love coming down here when you were little. I've still got all your toys and books over there."

I looked around the room. There really was nothing to hate. The walls were painted in a soft, yellow colour and the ceiling was covered in an enchanting, light blue one. There were a couple of sofas in the corners of the room which were perfect for curling up in with a good book. There was a play area where I'd spent many happy hours with myself and my imagination.

It wasn't the room's fault that I hated it. In fact, I didn't hate the room. I hated the memories associated with it.

But Gran didn't know about those memories. And I wasn't going to reveal them. Speaking about them would give them life. I didn't want that. I wanted to keep them hidden away at the very back of my mind. Maybe one day I'd forget about them altogether.

Gran was studying me. "I can see you've got something on your mind. You can tell me about it whenever you're ready." She began to walk to the other side of the room.

My heart missed a beat, and my voice caught in my throat as I said, "Gran, where are you going?"

Without looking over her shoulder, Gran replied, "You know where I'm going. You've been here before."

"No. Gran, no. Don't do it. I don't want to."

Gran stopped, turned around and said, "You have to. This is more important than you know. Come closer. Please."

"No." I clenched my hands at my side. My feet betrayed me. The sneaky things moved forward, and I couldn't stop them.

I came to a stop behind Gran and gave her a desperate look. "Please don't open that door."

"I have to," Gran said softly. "You've been through this door before. It's time you went through it again." She turned away from me and reached out for the brass handle of the wooden door in front of her.

My legs felt weak, and I closed my eyes. Damn! There was that fluttering butterfly in my stomach again. And it had brought a couple of friends with it who were having a merry dance in there. This wasn't the time to feel excited! This was the time to feel dread. To turn on my heel and run away. To jump in my car and race home. To leap into my bed, throw the covers over myself and pretend this door didn't exist.

The door let out a familiar creak, and my eyes shot open.

Gran pulled the door open towards us.

I rocked back on my feet as a wonderfully welcome aroma came towards me.

It was the smell of a spring morning when the first warm breeze hit you, and you knew winter had gone. It was also the crisp scent of winter when you knew snow was on its way. It was the exciting smell of summer as you opened your window on the first day of your school holidays. And it was the smoky fragrance of autumn as you noticed the first leaf turning colour.

Those dancing butterflies in my stomach went crazy and started flittering about all over the place. My heartbeat sped up and adrenaline coursed through me. I felt alive and ready for an adventure. I hadn't felt like this for years and years.

Gran took my hand, and we stepped through the door.

Once through the door, we were in another world. We walked along the cobbled road in front of us and looked at the town ahead.

Gran squeezed my hand and said, "Cassia, welcome back to Brimstone."

Chapter 4

Brimstone.

Yes. Of course.

I inhaled the refreshing air. I'd been here before. A long, long time ago. I looked at the town beyond the short, cobbled road. The brightly coloured buildings were set around a large square of grass. A white, wooden gazebo stood proudly in the middle of the grass and flowers adorned its rails and steps. Picnic tables and benches were dotted invitingly around the gazebo. I felt a pull towards them as if they were beckoning me to take a break from life. People wandered happily around the square, laughing and chatting to one another. Their clothes were so bright! All the colours of the rainbow and more.

When I say people, they weren't human beings. But I wasn't going to think about that at this moment. My mind was probably playing tricks on me, so I turned my attention away from the cloaked figure in the distance whose sharp fangs caught the sunlight. A vampire? No. Don't be silly. If he were a vampire, why would he be out in the bright sunshine? Of course, he wasn't a vampire. He was probably some poor soul who liked dressing up as one.

Gran tugged on my hand. "I don't think you're quite ready to meet the residents of Brimstone yet. Cassia, I know you haven't been here since you were a little girl, and your sensible grown-up mind is most likely telling you this is an illusion, but try to keep an open mind." She broke into a grin, and her eyes glittered with mischief. "Tell yourself you're on a drug-induced trip.

Convince yourself I slipped something herby into your tea and we're on an imaginary adventure together."

"I wouldn't put it past you to slip something into my tea," I mumbled. I pressed my lips together and looked at the beautiful tree to my left. The sun shone through the pale green and yellow leaves making them almost translucent. "Gran, I do remember being here. I remember this tree. And all the others like it dotted around the town. Why do I remember them? Why are they so special?"

Gran's grin broadened and she looked like the Cheshire Cat. "I'm so glad you remember the trees. Watch this."

She released my hand and then held both of her hands palms up towards the tree. She gave a soft whistle. There was a rustling sound and two leaves floated away from the tree. The leaves opened up, fluttered towards Gran and landed softly on her palms.

I smiled. "They're butterflies. They're so beautiful."

Gran held her left palm towards me. "This is the female one. Her wings are a pale green with a single red spot." She moved her right palm. "This one is the male. You can see that his wings are yellow. Like butter. It's thought that this is where the word 'butterfly' comes from. From this little chap."

The little butterfly opened and closed his wings as if to say, 'Yes, that's right.'

I gazed at the charming creatures and one by one, memories started to drop like soft snowflakes into my mind. I pointed to them and said, "They're Brimstone butterflies. This town is named after them. Am I right?"

Gran nodded. "Can you recall why the town is named after them?"

Another soft memory made itself known.

"Yes!" I declared. "The coven was looking for a new place to live, so they sent out many creatures to find a suitable area. The Brimstone butterflies found this area. It was perfect for the coven." My sudden joy abruptly vanished. "Wait. Did I just say coven? As in witches?"

"You did. And you're right. The Brimstone butterflies found this amazing place for the witches and as a thank you, the witches planted enchanted trees that would be perfect for the butterflies to live on. Such is the enchantment that anyone who attempts to hurt a Brimstone butterfly will immediately burst into flames." She smiled down at the male butterfly.

I snorted with disbelief. "Burst into flames? You're making that up."

Gran looked my way. "It's either burst into flames or turn into a pillar of dust. Either way, it's the end for whoever hurts the butterfly." She winked at me. "That's what we tell everyone."

Gran lowered her head and spoke quietly to the butterfly in her right hand. The butterfly flapped its wings twice and then flew away. The female butterfly returned to her position on the tree. The other leaves, which I now knew were green and yellow butterflies, shimmered as she returned. It was like they were welcoming her back.

I sighed. It must be wonderful to have hundreds of creatures welcoming you back home. All I had was a death-obsessed skinny cat.

"Gran, what did you say to that butterfly?"

"I gave him a message, of course," she said matter-of-factly.

"Right. Of course. Yep. I do that all the time." I took a step away from Gran.

Gran shook her head in exasperation. "Cassia, don't tell me you've forgotten what the butterflies do? They don't just hang around looking pretty on the trees. For goodness' sake! You must remember. After what you and Luca did."

Luca?

My heart stopped for a second.

Luca. I knew that name.

Gran continued, "The butterflies take messages. Rather like texting but much more pleasing to the eye. You summon a butterfly, tell it your message and who the message is going to, and then off it flies. It can either whisper your message to the recipient. Or it can sing it or shout it depending on what you asked it to do. Some of the shyer butterflies let the words appear on their wings. It's an excellent system and 100% efficient. Cassia, you must remember."

I looked at the tree. The butterflies fluttered slightly, and I felt like they were looking at me. A slow smile spread across my face. Yes. I did remember. How could I forget the messages I used to send using this amazing system. And that one time when Luca and I …

Heat flooded my cheeks, and I quickly looked away from the butterflies.

"Yes. You've remembered the butterflies alright," Gran said. "It looks like you've also remembered what you and Luca did."

A shadow suddenly fell over me, and a male voice boomed out, "Did someone mention my name?" This was followed by a warm chuckle which sent shivers down my spine.

I looked up into the face of the most handsome man I'd ever seen. And I'd watched a lot of TV. He had short, brown hair and the most incredible blue eyes I'd ever gazed at. They were a deep blue, like the ocean or a ripe blueberry. Or those chewy sweets that I had when I was little. I'd always loved those blue ones. And my pendant! I had a pendant with a crystal the exact same colour. I couldn't tear my gaze away from this perfect vision in front of me. Could he be any more handsome?

Then he smiled. Oh. He had dimples. Cute little dimples that I wanted to touch. My hand raised of its own accord.

The man abruptly pulled me into his embrace, lifted me off the ground and swung me around. I suddenly became a wanton woman and rested my head against his chest. He smelled warm and familiar. He smelled of home. I didn't know who he was, but I was enjoying this contact. My arms tightened around his waist, and I didn't care that I was acting like a hussy.

Gran coughed politely.

The man put me down, moved me to arm's-length and looked me up and down. "Cassia Winter, I haven't seen you since you were seven years old. You're all grown up. Wow. You're beautiful. I didn't think it was possible for you to get even more beautiful." He reached out and gently touched the end of my nose. "You've still got that freckle there. I'm glad you've still got it."

I wrinkled my nose. That annoying freckle! I covered it up with concealer every morning. The make-up must have worn off. It's hard to look like a tough, business woman when you've got a big, fat freckle on the end of your nose which makes you look like a twelve-year-old girl.

The man tilted his head to one side. His smile faltered. "Cassia? You don't remember me, do you?"

It was my turn to look him up and down. I took my time over it and admired his lean physique. I didn't know what had come over me. I never eyed men up like this.

My attention landed on his face. I smiled at him. "Luca. You're Luca. We used to play together."

Luca clapped his hands together and let out a loud laugh. "Yes! We did! We were best friends. Do you remember when we …?" He waggled his eyebrows and looked towards the butterfly tree.

My cheeks warmed up again, and my hand covered my mouth. My eyes were wide as I tried to stifle my laugh.

Gran tapped her foot. "What you two did was not funny. You caused chaos that day. And it was weeks before those poor butterflies recovered." She tutted several times, but I saw the twinkle in her eyes.

Luca lifted his chin. "We were performing a scientific experiment, weren't we, Cassia?"

My hand dropped, and I lifted my chin too. "Yes, we were. It was an extremely important experiment. We wanted to know how many messages the butterflies could deliver in one day."

"And how many messages they could remember at one time," Luca added. "Also, we needed to know in how many different forms they could deliver those messages. I was in charge of the whispering and talking as I gave the messages."

"And I was in charge of the singing, shouting and screaming," I finished. "It took us ages to give messages to each butterfly and to make sure everyone in the town got at least a dozen messages."

Luca gave me a wicked smile. "But it was worth it. Do you remember, Cassia, how the town looked when the butterflies all set off at once? It was magical."

I looked towards the town. "It was like the town was made up of flying leaves. It was awesome."

"It wasn't awesome at all," Gran said loudly. "It was chaos. I got two hundred messages that day, and all from different butterflies. By the end of the day, those poor creatures didn't know if they were coming or going. And it didn't help when people chased after them and asked them to repeat the first message they'd received."

Luca pressed his lips tightly together, but the laughter in his eyes gave him away.

I couldn't help myself. I burst into laughter. That wonderful, uncontrollable laughter that makes your cheeks hurt and your stomach ache.

Luca joined in with my laughter, and there was a mixture of guffaws and snorts as we let the laughter out. I wasn't sure if the snorts came from me or Luca. I'll blame him. I'm too much of a lady to snort so loudly.

It was a good five minutes before we got ourselves under control.

When we did, Luca wiped his tears of joy away and said to me, "I've waited years for you to return. I knew you would one day. Well, you had to, didn't you? Now that your gran is – "

Gran swiftly interrupted him, "Luca, it's been lovely to see you, but we have to get going." She took a step forward.

Confusion crossed Luca's face. "Cassia, you have come back, haven't you? You have come back to help your gran? Haven't you?"

Gran's tone was stern as she said, "Luca, a decision hasn't been made yet. We're going to see Blythe. We must get going. I can't keep her waiting."

Luca hadn't finished. "Cassia, promise me that you'll help. This town needs you. And your gran needs you."

Gran pulled on my arm and dragged me away. I had no idea she was so strong. Her grip stayed vice-like on my arm as she steered me away from Luca.

I glanced over my shoulder as I was frog-marched away. I gave Luca a helpless look along with a small smile.

He didn't return my smile. He folded his arms and watched us walk away.

"That was rude," I said to Gran.

"We haven't got time to chat. Blythe is waiting for us. You do remember Blythe, don't you?"

My heart sank all the way down to my feet, and they felt like lead as I was forced down the street. "Yes, I remember Blythe."

Chapter 5

Blythe was a three-hundred-year-old witch. She was in charge of Brimstone. She ruled with a steely-eyed fairness. She never missed a trick. She always knew when someone was up to no good.

Unfortunately.

It had been Blythe who'd discovered Luca and I were behind the butterfly incident. She'd reprimanded us in front of the town. I still remembered the deep shame of it. I had trembled in front of her, but Luca had held my hand throughout the ordeal. Blythe gave us our punishment in front of the town too. We had to go around to each and every citizen and apologise profusely for all the messages we'd sent via the butterflies. There were hundreds of citizens, and it took us days.

If that wasn't bad enough, we had to then apologise to each and every butterfly. There were thousands of butterflies. But we had to deal with our punishment and Luca and I tirelessly started our apologies. We'd been saying sorry for two straight days, and my voice was barely audible. Blythe must have felt sorry for us at that stage. She told us to apologise to the butterfly trees one-by-one rather than the individual butterflies. There are fifty-five butterfly trees in Brimstone Vale. I've talked to the residents of each one personally.

My mouth lifted slightly at one side. It had been worth it. Luca and I had sat inside the gazebo that wonderful day when the butterfly chaos happened. We laughed until we gave ourselves stomach ache.

Gran nudged me. "Take that guilty look off your face. I don't know what you're thinking about, but I'll bet it's nothing good."

I immediately straightened my lips into a thin, serious line.

We walked along the street and turned left at the first crossing. A huge house faced us. It was Blythe's house. It was the largest building in Brimstone. One of the perks of being in charge, I suppose.

Blythe's house is built of red brick with a pale red-tiled roof. I don't know what the bricks were made of but tiny flecks of gold shone out and it gave the house a shimmering look, almost like a heat shimmer. The house had a dreamlike aspect as if it was a figment of your imagination and could disappear in the blink of an eye. I suppose that's one of the benefits of being a three-hundred-year-old witch. You could have a magical house that sparkles and twinkles.

You'd think a three-hundred-year-old witch would be as wrinkled as a prune. Perhaps with a bowed back and an evil glint in her beady eye. Maybe she'd have the obligatory green wart on the end of her nose, complete with a few stiff hairs on her chin.

Blythe isn't like that.

The door to the twinkly house opened, and Blythe stepped out. I was immediately reminded of how mouth-droppingly beautiful she is. If that's even an expression. But that's what happens when people meet her for the first time. Their mouths drop open and their eyes widen as if they're unable to take in her beauty. Blythe has long, raven-black hair which flows over her shoulders in perfect waves. Her skin is radiant, and her plump mouth is always ready to smile – although, she didn't smile when she told Luca and me off. She's tall and slim and wears flowing clothes in many shades of purple. To match her eyes. Yes, she's got purple eyes. A light, beautiful shade of purple.

Those purple eyes now twinkled at me as she came to a stop. Her voice was warm as she said, "Cassia. You're a wonderful sight for sore eyes. My! Look at how you've grown. You're almost as tall as me." She studied me closer and then turned to look at Gran. "Esther, you were right about her. You were right to bring her here."

Gran gave Blythe a slight incline of her head. "I should have brought her here years ago. I just hope it's not too late."

"Too late for what?" I asked.

Blythe turned her purple eyes my way. She put her arm around my shoulder. "We'll discuss this inside. You never know who's listening to our conversation."

I looked behind me half expecting to see a group of people with their heads cocked in our direction. The only person I saw was a slim man with extremely pointy ears. He looked like an elf. Or some foolish man trying to look like an elf.

Blythe led us up the glittering path and into her house.

As soon as I entered, something weird happened to me. An enormous variety of memories swooped into my head. One by one. One after the other. Thud. Thud. Thud.

Severe pain accompanied each memory and I let out a cry. It was a good job Blythe still had her arm around me, otherwise I would have collapsed to the floor when my knees gave way.

Blythe caught me in my faint, whipped me into her arms as if I weighed nothing, and took me into her large living room. She settled me on the sofa in a half-sitting position.

Blythe placed a hand on my forehead and said to someone behind her, "Pink lemonade, Brin, please. And quickly. Thank you."

Brin. I knew that name. I flinched as another memory crashed into my brain.

Blythe smoothed my hair back. "Let the memories come, Cassia. Let them in. Don't fight them. This will be over before you know it."

"But it hurts," I said. I could feel tears rolling down my cheeks. I felt stupid for crying over such a silly thing. But it really did hurt.

Gran pulled a padded stool over to the sofa and sat down. She took my hand and said, "You've been suppressing the memories for too long. This is all my fault. I should have done something about this years ago. I should have reminded you of your true nature. Look what I've done to you. You're a mess! A broken, crying mess."

"Thanks," I muttered. A fresh spasm of pain attacked me. It was like someone had opened my skull up and was dropping sharp bits of plastic into it.

There was the sound of feet walking into the room, an exchange of quiet words and then a glass of something pink and bubbly was pushed towards me from Blythe.

"Drink this," she ordered.

I did so. An immediate feeling of peace came over me. The pain vanished, and I blinked in surprise. I took another drink, and a happy feeling bubbled in my stomach. I smacked my lips together and was about to take another drink when Blythe whipped the glass away.

I reached out for it. "I'd like some more, please."

Blythe shook her head. "Brin must have made it extra strong. It's got herbs and a secret ingredient in it. You've had more than enough."

Gran looked at the glass and said to Blythe, "Is the secret ingredient gin?"

"No, vodka. I ran out of gin last week." Blythe turned to someone at her side. "Thank you, Brin. Keep this for later. I might have it as my nightcap."

I sat up straighter. "Brin! I remember." I moved my head so I could see the small creature at Blythe's side. I waved to the elf who was dressed in brown clothes and a white apron. "Hi, Brin! It's me, Cassia. Hi! You're a house Brownie. You work for Blythe! Hi!"

Brin gave me a shy wave.

Blythe said, "Brin doesn't work for me, she works with me. Cassia, you're very loud all of a sudden."

I flapped my hand at Brin. "You told me about being a house Brownie when I was little. You told me how they sneak into people's houses in the middle of the night to clean up. Ha! I wish I had a house Brownie in my apartment." I made a shushing motion and whispered loudly, "Brin, come home with me. I'll look after you. I know where all the best pizza takeaway places are."

Gran made a clicking noise with her tongue. "Cassia, you're drunk. Blythe, how much vodka was in that drink?"

I swung my feet off the sofa and grinned at Blythe. "I remember everything! Absolutely everything!" I jabbed a finger at her. "I remember you. And Brin. And Gran." I hiccupped. "Of course I remember Gran. I never forgot Gran. I love you, Gran."

"That's nice to know," Gran leant over and patted my hand. "There's no need to shout."

I got unsteadily to my feet and looked towards the large window at the front of the room. I could see the town square and the gazebo. I could see the residents clearly now.

I pointed at the window. "This town is full of supernatural beings! Gran, did you know that? I can see a vampire and a werewolf. They're having a chat. That's nice, isn't it? I can see a minotaur. He's got huge shoulders. And there's a unicorn prancing down the road. Wow. What a beautiful unicorn. And I can see little fairies flying around." I squinted. "I'm not sure what that creature is with two heads. Hello!" I waved at the creature in question.

"Cassia! Stop making an exhibition of yourself," Gran called out. She stood up and reached out a hand to me. She wobbled on her feet, and her other hand came out to steady herself. Pain crossed her face, and both hands went to her chest. The colour drained from her cheeks, and she collapsed back on to the stool.

I was immediately sober. Blythe and I rushed to Gran's side.

Blythe said to Brin, "Get the room ready."

Brin nodded and scampered away.

I looked at Blythe and said, "What's wrong with Gran? You know what's wrong. I can see it in your face. You have to tell me."

Gran muttered, "Blythe, don't tell her."

"Esther, I have to. You know that."

Gran flinched as she slowly shook her head. "You can't tell her. She's not ready."

"Stop talking about me as if I'm not here," I said more roughly than I meant to. "Gran, tell me what's wrong with you."

Chapter 6

Blythe said, "I'll tell you what's wrong with your gran. She's been working too hard, and she hasn't rested when she needed to. Just like you. You Winter witches are the most stubborn witches I've ever met. And I've met thousands of witches."

I was about to argue that I wasn't a witch and that I didn't believe in that sort of thing, but I didn't say the words. I knew without a doubt that I was a witch and that Gran was too. It was like a veil of lies had been lifted from my mind as soon as I stepped into Blythe's home. I'd been lying about my true nature for years, just like Gran said. What a waste of my years. But this wasn't the time to wallow in self-pity.

I gave Gran a loving look. "Why didn't you tell me you were doing too much? I could have helped you with the housework and the garden. I would have done all the shopping for you and all that volunteer work you do."

Blythe said, "Cassia, I'm not talking about her work in your world. Although, it does sound as if she's doing too much there too. I'm talking about the witch work she does here. She takes on enough work for three witches, maybe even four."

"Somebody has to do it," Gran said through clenched teeth. "I might need some of that pink lemonade."

"What kind of witch work?" I asked. "I don't understand."

Brin came running back into the room. "The room is ready for Esther."

"I'll tell you everything in a minute," Blythe said to me. "Let's get your gran sorted out first." She reached into her pocket. I wasn't entirely surprised to see her retrieve a slim wand. It was the same purple as her eyes.

She aimed her wand at Gran, and her eyes narrowed slightly.

Gran let out a sigh of relief and said, "Thank you. The pain has gone."

I said to Blythe, "What did you do? Did you put a spell on her? Did you use magic? You must have. Aren't you supposed to use magic words? Something in Latin?"

"Shh. I haven't finished yet." Blythe gently raised her wand while keeping her attention on Gran.

Gran moved upwards. Her legs were bent as if she was still sitting on the stool. As she moved higher, I could see the stool was still on the ground. I blinked. Seeing your gran floating in mid-air wasn't something you saw every day.

Gran winked at me. "Look, Cassia, I'm as light as a feather. Move out of the way."

I did so and watched in astonishment as Gran floated past me. "Where are you going?" I asked.

Blythe answered on Gran's behalf, "To the recovery room. Brin's got all sorts of lotions and potions in there. Things that will take away years of stress from your gran. She'll be a new woman when Brin's finished with her."

Gran ruffled my hair as she went past. "Don't look so worried. I've been in the recovery room before. It's wonderful. Brin's potions are amazing. I'll try and smuggle us some out." She winked again before floating out of the room. Brin walked after her.

Blythe held her wand up for a few more seconds and then lowered it. "Esther's in the room now. All her cares and woes will be gone in minutes along with her aches and pains. If only I could do something with that stubborn streak of hers."

"Can't you use magic on her stubborn streak?"

"Not on Esther. She's too strong-willed. Like you. Take a seat. We need to talk. Are you hungry? I am."

Blythe sat in the middle of the sofa and flicked her wand at the empty table in front of her. A selection of delicious-looking food appeared on the table. Sandwiches and cakes, scones and crisps, cucumber slices and thick chunks of chocolate. Saliva rushed into my mouth, and a tiny bit of drool escaped. A pot of tea appeared at the side of the food with two flower patterned cups.

I wiped the drool from my mouth and sat next to Blythe. My stomach rumbled, but I said, "The food looks lovely, but no, thank you. I'm not hungry."

"Your stomach is telling me something different." Blythe hooked a finger under a strand of my hair and lifted it towards her nose. She sniffed it. "What sort of food have you been eating? Gluten-free. Fat-free. No wheat. No sugar. Low sodium." She dropped my hair. "Why are you eating that kind of food?"

"I've got allergies," I defended myself.

"No, you haven't."

I tried another tactic. "Everyone eats like that. You have to watch what you eat. There's all sorts of hidden stuff in food these days." I pointed at the food in front of me. "There's loads of sugar in that chocolate. And I haven't had white bread in over a year."

Blythe shook her head. "Why would you deny yourself such a treat? I don't eat this kind of food all the time, but a treat now and then does you good."

My stomach rumbled again. Traitor. I looked away from the food.

Blythe said, "Would you eat it if I made it compatible with your so-called allergies?"

I looked back at her. "Possibly."

Blythe aimed her wand at the food. After two seconds she said, "There we are. It's safe to eat. And there are barely any calories in it so you can go mad and stuff your face. Tea?"

"Yes, please." I was already reaching for a cheese sandwich. I shoved it in my mouth. My tongue tingled with joy, and I closed my eyes to appreciate the savoury taste of the cheese and the softness of the bread. The suspicious side of my brain said Blythe could be lying about changing the food. But the other part of my brain said it didn't care and pass me a chunk of chocolate.

I was soon stuffing my face, and for five minutes I completely forgot about my worn-out gran. When I did remember her, my eating slowed down, and I reached for the cup of tea that Blythe had poured for me.

I said, "Shall we check on Gran now?"

Blythe tilted her head and listened to silence for a moment. "No, she's already recovering." She picked up her cup of tea and gave me her full attention. "We'll talk more about your gran soon. First, I want to hear about you and your life. Although your gran talks about you all the time, I'd rather hear from you about how things are. Begin." She took a sip of her tea.

I took a sip of my tea too and then said, "Begin where?"

Blythe lowered her cup. "At the beginning, of course. Start from when we last saw each other. That would be shortly after the incident with the butterflies."

My cheeks flushed warm again. I didn't know I could feel embarrassed so many times, and over the same incident too.

Blythe's gaze went to my pink cheeks and she smiled. "Cassia, there's no need to feel embarrassed. It was quite funny. Not at the time, but afterwards. I never got the chance to tell you what happened as a result of your little prank with Luca."

I put my cup back on the table. "I know what happened. I nearly lost my voice apologising to everyone."

"You actually did some of the residents a favour."

"How?"

"Well, you made sure that every citizen got at least a dozen messages. Some of our more reserved and lonely citizens barely get one message a year, so for them to get a flurry of butterfly messages all in one day was a great gift. Even the grumpy dwarf who lives two mountains away was happy. He actually smiled. I didn't think he could smile."

"Oh, that's nice," I said.

"And that's not all," Blythe continued. "Each and every butterfly was in action that day. Some of the shyer ones don't often take messages and they hide in the middle of the tree where no one can see them. They all got out that day, and even though some of them grumbled about being exhausted by the evening, they had a marvellous time. They still talk about that day. I think they've even made a song up about it."

I settled back on the sofa. "So, Luca and I did the town a favour."

"Don't look so smug. You didn't intend to do us a favour, and you know that." Blythe put her cup down. "Why did you stop your visits to our town? I haven't seen you since you were seven."

My eyes stung, and I looked down at my jean-clad knees. "I don't want to talk about it."

"Yes, I can see that. But I need to know." She shuffled along the sofa. "If you'll allow me, I can look at the memories inside your head, and that will save you having to vocalise them."

I looked at her. "How do you do that? Are you going to aim your wand at me? Are you going to stick it in my ear or something?"

"Goodness me! Of course not. I don't need to use my wand at all when I do magic. But it's a beautiful wand, and I do like to show it off." She rubbed her palms together. "I simply put my hands on your temples. It doesn't hurt."

"Do you really need to know?"

"I do. Please, Cassia. I think it would help you to share those memories too."

I quickly blinked my tears away and gave her a nod.

Blythe put her palms against my temples and told me to focus on the reasons why I hadn't returned to Brimstone. It didn't take long for those particular thoughts to come to my mind. I wished there was a way to get rid of them forever, but I knew I never would.

Blythe held her hands gently against my head for about a minute. Her hands were warm, and my eyelids began to feel heavy.

Blythe took her hands away. There were tears in her eyes. "Oh, Cassia, you poor thing. I didn't realise. I should have worked it out. You were seven when your mum went away. And the last time you saw her was when she went through your gran's cellar door and came here. I saw you sitting in the cellar waiting for her. You were crying and calling out for her."

I said, "She told me to wait by the door for her. So I did. I waited and waited. But she never came back. Even when Gran told me Mum wouldn't be coming back, I still waited. I went into that cellar every day. I kept myself busy while I waited. I drew lots of pictures for Mum, and I read loads of books. It took me a long time to realise she wouldn't be coming back. That's when I decided I'd never go into Gran's cellar again. And I'd never go back to Brimstone. I blamed this town for taking Mum away." Tears were rolling down my cheeks, but I couldn't stop them.

Blythe nodded. "I totally understand. We have missed you. The whole town has missed you. You were such a breath of fresh air. Cassia, I caught some of your other memories while I was in your head. You're not happy. You're miserable in your job, and you dread waking up each morning. It feels like you're dying from the inside out. And what's all this about Stanley and funeral caskets?"

I wiped my tears away. It was one emotion after the other today. I wasn't used to it. "I don't want to talk about my life anymore. What's going on with Gran? You said you'd tell me."

Blythe gave me a slow nod. "I did. Okay. Esther does work for this town. She takes care of any lawbreakers."

"Lawbreakers? She's like the police?"

"Sort of. We don't have an official police force here. Everything is governed by the witches. Each coven has its own department. We have the health and healing witches, the environmental witches, the town and planning witches. You get the idea. The Winter witches take care of our justice system. Your mum used to do that too. We don't have a lot of crime in this town, but when we do, Esther is the one who investigates it."

I smiled. "That explains it. Gran's obsessed with police and mystery shows. She's got dozens and dozens of box sets. She loves watching Poirot, Miss Marple and Murder, She Wrote. Amongst many others."

Blythe continued, "The Winter witches have special abilities. They're observant and have a good instinct for how people behave. Or should I say, how supernatural creatures behave. Esther, in particular, is incredibly persistent when she has a case to deal with. She won't rest until the mystery is solved."

"I had no idea she was doing this. Why didn't she ever tell me?"

"She couldn't. You made it clear to her that you didn't want to know what went on in Brimstone."

I lowered my head as guilt rushed through me. "Poor Gran. Has she been very busy with her work?"

"She has. She refuses to let anyone help her. She's said that she'll only accept help from another Winter witch. That's you, Cassia. You have to help Esther before she collapses from exhaustion."

"How can I do that? I have a job. I can't just leave it. I have responsibilities. I've only just remembered that I'm a witch. I need time to process that. Does Gran use her witch powers when she's working? Would I have to use my powers? I don't even know what my powers are. I don't even have a wand! Or a pointy hat!" I started to hyperventilate.

Blythe placed a hand on my shoulder, and my breathing returned to normal. Blythe said, "I can help you with the witch part. I'll train you. You don't need a pointy hat, not unless you feel the need to wear one. Cassia, I'm not asking you to make a decision at this very moment. But you do need to think about it. Being a witch is what you are meant to be. And – "

"Don't say another word," Gran said as she walked into the room. "I don't need any help. I'm as fit as a fiddle." She hitched her tweed skirt up and jigged from side to side. "I'm as strong as an ox. Look." She held her arm out as if flexing her muscle. Her cardigan sleeve didn't move.

Blythe said, "Esther, Brin's potions won't last for long. You need help with your justice work. You know you do. Cassia can help you."

"Nonsense. Cassia's got her own life to lead. She's got responsibilities. I don't need her help. I don't need anyone's help." Gran had that determined look on her face that I'd seen many times. It was the look that said, 'Don't even think about arguing with me.'

Blythe stood up and held her hands out. "Esther, please think about this."

"I have thought about it," Gran said. "I've made my decision. Cassia, we're going home. You can go back to your job and forget all about being a witch. You can put all thoughts of Brimstone right out of your head. It's time for you to return to your normal life."

Chapter 7

Gran almost pulled my arm out of its socket as she dragged me out of Blythe's house. I managed to give the confused-looking Blythe a swift goodbye before being pulled out of the door and along the path.

Gran sped up as she forced me down the street and towards the cobbled road in front of the cellar door.

"Gran, wait!" I protested as I was propelled along.

Gran was having none of it. The determined set of her chin was a familiar sight.

As we went through the door, I was vaguely aware of someone shouting my name. Luca? I looked over my shoulder as we went through the opening. Before I had the chance to search for Luca, the cellar door was slammed shut behind us.

"Here we are," Gran said. She gave me a sharp nod. "Back where you belong. We'll have no more talk of Brimstone and witches. Haven't you got somewhere to be? Haven't you got some paperwork to do? Off you go then." She put her hand on my elbow and steered me towards the cellar steps.

I shrugged free. "Gran, I can manage to walk without you pushing and shoving me. Why did we leave Blythe's house so abruptly? We didn't even say thank you. And I could have sworn I heard Luca calling my name. I wanted to talk to him again."

"There's no point. You won't be seeing Luca or Blythe ever again." She marched over to the steps and began to ascend them.

I ran after her. "But Gran! Blythe told me you need help. I want to help you. I want to learn more about being a witch."

"No!" Gran spun around so quickly I was afraid she was going to topple down the steps. She pointed a finger at me. "You don't belong there. It's too dangerous. I won't lose you like I lost your – " She took a sharp intake of breath. "Cassia, I had no right telling you about this witch business. My life and work in Brimstone have nothing to do with you. You've managed this long without remembering you're a witch, and you can continue to do so." She turned back around and finished climbing the steps. She disappeared through the door.

I raced after her. "But what about my health? You said my health was suffering because I was suppressing my true nature." I ran through the door. "Gran, talk to me. Why don't you want me to help you?"

Gran was standing at the other side of the kitchen. She was holding the door open with one hand, and my handbag was in her other. Oliver was at her side, his head bowed and his gaze averted.

Talk about feeling unwelcome.

Gran held my handbag up. "It's been lovely to see you, but I have a million and one things to do. I won't see you to your car. Goodbye. Thanks for visiting."

Her forced smile wasn't something I'd seen aimed in my direction before. My throat felt tight, and my words wouldn't come out. I took my handbag, gave her a small nod and walked out of the kitchen and into the garden.

My vision swam with unshed tears as I walked to my car. I'm not entirely sure how I managed to drive in my confused state, but I must have because twenty minutes later I was pulling into the underground car park of my apartment building.

I was still feeling numb as I let myself into my modern-looking apartment. I closed the door, dropped my handbag and leant back against the door. I let the tears flow freely.

Gran had never, ever been that abrupt with me before. What had I done to upset her? What had happened to her when she went into that recovery room with Brin? Had she had a brain transplant?

A quiet voice at the back of my mind told me Gran's sudden change of mind had nothing to do with me. She was trying to protect me in the best way she could. I ignored the voice; it was far too sensible. And I wanted to feel sorry for myself for a while.

I walked over to the kettle and filled it with water. I called out for Stanley, but he didn't appear. I hoped he wasn't attending another funeral.

I recalled the happy feelings that had swept over me when I'd walked into Brimstone. It was home. It was welcoming. I belonged there. Luca's face flashed into my mind, and I smiled. I so wanted to talk to him again. And I wanted to know more about being a witch. I wanted to have long talks with Blythe.

I picked a mug up from the draining board, and my hand clenched around it. A spurt of anger burst through me. I slammed the mug down and cried out, "Damn it! I want to be a witch! I want to go back to Brimstone! I want to help Gran!"

Just as swiftly, the anger was gone. I checked the mug and was glad to see it was still intact. Phew. It was my favourite mug. It had the name of one of my favourite TV shows on it: *Supernatural*. I loved that show. It was all about creatures from fantasy and fiction: werewolves, vampires, ghosts, demons. I also loved watching *Buffy, The Vampire Slayer, The Vampire Diaries and Teen Wolf*.

Yes, there was a theme here.

As I waited for the kettle to boil, I looked around my neat and compact apartment. Everything here was in varying shades of grey. It was the complete opposite of Gran's house. There was nothing in my living space that was considered frivolous and ornamental. Everything had a purpose. Alastair had helped me to decorate it. He had good taste. He said the apartment should have a neutral look so that when it was time for me to sell it, potential buyers wouldn't be put off by my personality stamped all over it.

Alastair had also helped me find this apartment. It was a good investment, so he'd said. In an up-and-coming part of town. I would make a good profit when it was time to move on. I'd agreed with him even though I'd rather live in a home and make it mine than live in a grey, investment property.

The kettle boiled and I made myself a coffee.

Alastair Smith. My boyfriend of three years. We'd met at the insurance company where we both still worked. He'd been my supervisor and had given me considered feedback on my work. If he was harsh, he said it was because he could see the potential in me. He'd got promoted and moved to a different department, but he still made sure he could be my mentor. It worked because I was soon promoted too. When he asked me out, it seemed impolite to refuse after all he'd done for me.

I wonder what Alastair would think about me being a witch? I smiled to myself. I knew exactly what he'd think. Stuff and nonsense. Hocus-pocus hogwash. A load of old codswallop. He didn't understand why I liked watching supernatural shows, and he voiced his opinion loudly every time his attention landed on my box set collection. Needless to say, I watched those shows on my own.

As if knowing I was thinking about him, my phone beeped and a text came through from Alastair:

'Hope you've done those staff appraisals by now. Email them to me. I'll edit them and add my opinions. A'

No X at the end of the text. No note of affection in his words.

I scowled at the message. Alastair had nothing to do with the staff appraisals. They were my responsibility. He only wanted to look at them because he liked to control me.

Whoa. I'd never thought of Alastair in that way before. He cared about my career, that's why he wanted to look at the appraisals. He didn't want me to make any professional mistakes. He cared about me. He loved me.

Does he? That treacherous voice was back in my head. I put the phone down. I didn't trust myself to reply at the moment. Part of me wanted to tell Alastair where he could shove the appraisals.

What had come over me? I never had thoughts like this.

I took my coffee over to the small desk in the corner of the living room. This was my office area. Alastair insisted I have one so that I could maintain a professional attitude when I worked through my weekends –unpaid, I might add.

I paused by the desk fully intending to sit down and do those stupid appraisals. My feet thought otherwise and carried me through to my small bedroom. I stopped next to the wardrobe and placed my coffee on the light grey carpet. I opened the wardrobe door and sank to my knees. I reached towards the box that was hidden at the back beneath a blanket. I knew looking at it would only bring me heartbreak, but I knew I had to.

I pulled the box out, sat back on the carpet and looked at the lid. My childish writing noted the items inside the box as 'Things To Show Mum When She Comes Back.'

I hadn't looked inside this box for years. Not since I'd finally realised Mum wasn't coming back. I frowned as I thought about that time. Had there been a funeral? I couldn't remember one. Perhaps I didn't go. Or perhaps

I'd fully blocked the painful memories from my mind. I was good at blocking memories.

I took the lid off and carefully took the contents out. I laid them on the carpet and began to look through them.

Lots of drawings and paintings. Lots of little notes telling Mum what I'd done at school that day. Many, many heart-shaped notes telling Mum that I loved her and I hoped she'd come back soon.

The paintings showed Mum and me together. Gran was in some of them. I found pictures I'd drawn of a small boy with dark blue eyes. Luca? We were holding hands and chasing green butterflies down a street. I'd attempted to draw something that looked like a vampire. Or a werewolf. Or a cloud with legs. It was hard to make out. I turned the drawing around and squinted at it. An elf?

A sudden thudding at the front door made me drop the picture. My heart sped up.

Alastair? Somehow, he must know that I hadn't done the appraisals yet. I could ignore him, but he'd know I was inside. He'd put one of those 'find my friend' apps on my phone so he always knew where I was. For my own safety, he'd explained to me.

The thudding came again. It sounded angry.

I dragged myself over to the door and tried to come up with excuses as to why I was behind with my work. That defiant voice in my head shouted, 'Tell him it's Sunday! You don't do office work on a Sunday! Tell him to get a life!'

I slowly opened the door.

It wasn't Alastair standing there.

Chapter 8

"Is this your cat?"

I looked at the short, elderly woman in front of me. Her face was pale, and her eyes were red-rimmed from crying. She wasn't the first bereaved person to turn up at my door. My glance went to the grey-haired cat in her arms.

"Yes," I replied. "Sorry for any inconvenience he's caused you."

The woman tickled Stanley behind his ears. "Inconvenience? He hasn't been an inconvenience at all. In fact, he's been a great comfort to me today."

"Has he?"

Stanley hadn't met my gaze yet. He was staring intently at the woman's sleeve as if he knew I was looking at him.

"Yes." The woman chuckled. "I buried my Arthur today. We'd been married sixty years. I wasn't sure how I was going to get through today."

"I'm sorry for your loss. I hope today hasn't been too upsetting for you."

"Upsetting? No. You've got me wrong. I wasn't upset that Arthur had gone. He was a miserable, old trout and I'm glad to see the back of him. He made my life a misery. He complained non-stop about every little thing you could imagine. Everyone hated him. He didn't have any friends. Even his mother didn't like him." She tickled Stanley again and smiled.

My brow wrinkled. "I'm confused. How was Stanley a comfort to you if you weren't upset about your husband passing on?"

"Because I was the only one at the church service. Well, besides the vicar and the undertakers. I was so embarrassed! I thought his brothers might have turned up. At least to see the back of him. But no, it was just me. And then your lovely cat walked into the church. He gave me a nod as if to say hello and then he jumped up onto the coffin. He cheered me right up. Your cat must have known my Arthur. Perhaps he brought out a hidden kind side to him. Anyway, it was nice to have company. Your adorable cat stayed with me right through the service. He even refused to get off the coffin when it was taken to the cemetery. He rode in the hearse with it!"

I didn't have the heart to tell her he'd done that three times last week.

She continued, "I was a bit worried when he jumped into the hole after the coffin was lowered into the ground."

"Pardon? He jumped into the hole?" He'd never done that before.

Stanley twisted his head fully away from my searching look.

Great. Not only was my cat obsessed with death, he was now suicidal. Did cats get suicidal? If so, what do I do about it? I'd have to Google that later.

A concerned look crossed the woman's face and she said, "I hope you don't mind me saying so, but your cat is terribly thin. Is he ill? Has he seen a vet?"

"Yes, many times. The vet said he's in perfect health."

She took a step closer and looked over my shoulder into my apartment which I thought was a bit cheeky.

"You don't have a garden. And that's a very small space for a cat to run around in."

"I can assure you that there's more than enough room to swing a cat in," I said with a smile. I instantly regretted my quip as horror flashed in the woman's eyes.

She pulled Stanley protectively closer to her. "I would be happy to take Stanley off your hands. I have a large garden, and he'd have a wonderful time there." Her tone took an accusing turn as she added, "I'd soon fatten him up.

For a split-second, I was tempted. Then Stanley turned his head and looked at me. My heart melted as it always did with that skinny, grey-haired cat.

I held my hands out and said, "No, thank you. And thank you for bringing him back."

The woman looked briefly to her right to where the lift was. I thought she was going to make a run for it. She could try. But I'd go after her.

I gave a polite cough and pushed my hands out further. Stanley leapt from the woman's arms and into mine. Bless him. He even purred in delight. He hardly ever purred, so I knew he was putting on a show.

The woman said, "Are you sure you won't change your mind?" She gave me a look which lasted five seconds. I kept my eyes locked on hers. When it came to my cat, I wasn't a pushover.

"No. Never. Thanks again." I kicked the door shut, and for good measure, I bolted it.

I turned my attention to the creature in my arms. "Stanley, this has got to stop. You can't keep turning up to funerals, especially when you don't know the deceased. It's extremely bad manners."

Stanley's whiskers twitched, and he looked confused. Is it possible for a cat to look confused? Something else to add to my Google list.

His whiskers continued to twitch. He moved his head close to my cheek and sniffed me. I felt a little dab on my cheek. It felt like wet sandpaper.

"Hey! Stop licking me. I don't know what germs you've picked up from the cemetery."

Stanley leapt from my arms and ran into the bedroom. I went after him. He didn't normally run anywhere. He usually dragged his paws along as if walking was too much trouble for him.

I found him sitting next to the pile of drawings. His paw was on the one of Luca and me chasing butterflies. Stanley's ears were standing to attention, and he was purring so loudly that I felt the floor vibrate. He was like a feline pneumatic drill.

I put my hands over my ears. "Stanley! Shh! What's got into you?"

His purring stopped, and he moved his paw on to the next picture. And the next one. And the next. His little mouth opened, and he bared his teeth in what looked suspiciously like a smile.

Was he happy? Was my small, death-obsessed cat actually happy?

I went over to Stanley, knelt at his side and stroked his thin back. I remembered what Gran had said about Stanley being my familiar. Could it be true?

"Stanley, do you know about Brimstone? Do you know I'm a witch?"

Stanley moved closer to me and put his furry head against my arm. A soft purr came from him which sent goosebumps travelling up my arm.

I pulled him onto my knee. "I've been there today, Stanley. I'd forgotten I was a witch."

He gave me a look as if to say, 'Tell me everything.'

So, that's what I did. As I concluded I said, "Gran doesn't want me to help her. I won't be going back to Brimstone."

Stanley looked deeply into my eyes. I could sense the sadness in him. I felt just as sad.

"What am I going to do, Stanley?"

He slid off my knee, lay on his back and stuck all four paws in the air.

"Play dead? That's not the answer. I have to carry on." I gave him a little nudge to make sure he was only pretending. He rolled on to his paws. "We both have to carry on as before."

Stanley let out a little cat sigh, dragged his paws over to the corner of the room where a dead spider lay. He settled down and stared at it morosely.

I felt like doing the same.

Chapter 9

I felt like death warmed up as I sat in my corner office the next morning. I yawned for the one-hundredth time and blinked rapidly in an effort to wake myself up.

Last night had been strange. After the incident with my box of memories, Stanley had stayed lying in front of that dead spider for hours. I couldn't tempt him away even with his favourite food. He didn't budge when the theme tune to *Buffy, The Vampire Slayer* blasted out from the TV. He loves that programme, and always snuggles up to me on the sofa when it's on.

At one point last night, I got down on all fours and put my face next to his. I asked him what was wrong, but, of course, he didn't answer. If he was my familiar, he wasn't doing a good job of it. Or was it the other way around? Was I doing a terrible job of being his witch?

After unsuccessfully trying to coax Stanley away from the departed spider, I returned to the living room with the full intention of completing those staff appraisals. I wasn't going to rest until every last one was finished. Then I would email them to Alastair, wait for him to get back to me with his opinions and suggestions, and then I would rewrite them.

That was my intention.

That intention vanished as soon as I looked at them. Instead, I scowled at the files and put them underneath my desk so I couldn't see them.

Then I went to the fridge and got myself a glass of lovely wine. I found a pepperoni pizza in the freezer and shoved that in the oven. It said on the packet it was a pizza made for sharing. Well, I was going to share it with myself, so that was okay. It wasn't gluten-free, or anything else free, and it was just what I needed. Goodness knows how long it had been in the freezer, but it hadn't poisoned me.

Once my refreshments had been taken care of, I settled down on the sofa with *Buffy* and listened out for the patter of cat feet. The feet never came. I ended up spending the evening on my own, but I didn't mind. I had a lot of information to process.

I was still processing that information the following morning. I'd tried to ring Gran first thing. I didn't want us to be on bad terms. We never had been before, and I didn't like how things had ended with us yesterday.

Gran didn't answer when I phoned. I tried her landline and mobile and left messages on both.

Now, here I was, early Monday morning in my office, barely awake and those irritating staff appraisals piled up in front of me. I was living the wrong life. I could feel it. I put my head in my hands, and a wave of despair washed over me.

"Morning!" Alastair called out as he strode into my office.

My office door is usually open. The people I work with always give a polite knock before entering. Alastair never does. He swans in like he owns the place. It must have been my lack of sleep or the events of yesterday, but anger bubbled up inside me. I felt like I was a volcano getting ready to erupt. I gave him a tight-lipped smile.

Alastair plonked his rear end on the end of my desk.

How can I describe him? Average. Average build and height. Indistinctive features. An everyday-looking kind of person. If he was involved in a crime, witnesses would be stumped to give a description of him. Average would be the word they used most.

Alastair began, "I tried phoning you last night, but your phone wasn't on. Are you having problems with your service provider? You are using the one I recommended, aren't you? Did you remember to charge your phone?" He gave me a condescending smile. "I know how forgetful you are."

"I did charge it up. I always charge it up. I switched it off on purpose."

"Oh? Why? I needed to talk to you. I knew you were at home because I checked the app."

"I switched it off because I needed some peace and quiet," I replied as politely as I could.

"Peace and quiet? Why?" He glanced at the paperwork in front of me. "Ah, yes. You had to complete the appraisals. Let's have a look at them."

He lunged across the desk and picked up a couple of files before I could stop him. He opened the first one and confusion crossed his face. He looked at the second one. Confusion was quickly replaced by anger.

He flung the files back on the desk and folded his arms tightly. "Cassia, what the hell are you playing at? These should have been completed by now. What will the managers on the top floor say when they hear about this? I'll tell you what they'll say. They'll blame me for recommending you for your recent promotion. Some of them had their doubts about you, but I said you'd manage with my help. Well? What have you got to say for yourself?"

I couldn't say anything. But the volcano inside me was bubbling away.

Alastair threw his hands in the air and got to his feet. "You need to get this mess sorted out right away. Your bad performance reflects on me, and I'm not having it. I've worked too hard to reach my present position. I won't have your substandard workmanship affecting my future prospects." He looked me up and down. "And do something about your appearance. Have you even attempted to put any make-up on this morning?"

The volcano was nearing eruption. I was going to tell him exactly what I thought. I opened my mouth to let him have it.

He held a hand up and said, "I don't want any of your excuses. Get those appraisals completed immediately. Don't sit there looking stupid. They won't do themselves." He gave me a cold look before walking away.

As soon as he left my office, my anger deflated and I let out a long sigh. I sounded like a balloon being let down at the end of a party.

I pulled the files closer to me and placed my hands on top of them. Alastair was right. I should have done these last night. I'd let him down.

I opened the first one. Cheryl Atkins. I smiled. Cheryl was a lovely person. She had two young children, and she often looked like she hadn't slept through the night, but she was always cheerful. She worked incredibly hard, and I was going to give her a glowing report and a pay rise.

My right hand tingled as I thought about what I was going to say. Then something strange happened. Words began to form on the paper. The very words I intended to write.

I quickly pulled my hand away, and the writing stopped. What had just happened? Magic? Had my visit to Brimstone awoken some hidden powers inside me?

I shrugged. I didn't care why it was happening. I put my hand back and thought again about what I wanted to write. The words flowed swiftly on to the paper. There were no spelling mistakes, and the punctuation appeared in all the right places. It was awesome. It was magical. It was probably against some witchy rules to be doing magic in such an open place. I didn't care. I was having fun.

Cheryl's appraisal was soon finished. I mumbled to myself, "So, Alastair, these appraisals won't do themselves, will they? Ha! You're wrong. Hee hee."

I carried on with the rest of the paperwork, and it was all completed in twenty minutes. I leant back in my chair and was about to revel in smugness, but something stopped me.

A sudden, cold feeling of dread came crashing down on me. It was so sudden that it took my breath away. My stomach clenched, and my heart thudded against my ribcage.

Something was wrong. Something was terribly wrong. I leapt to my feet and looked out on to the office floor. Was someone in trouble? Was someone hurt? I couldn't see anything.

My attention was drawn to a small green thing fluttering in the air. It headed towards me. As it came closer I saw what it was - a Brimstone butterfly.

How had it got into the building? All the windows were sealed shut. And why was no one else looking at it as it flew through the air?

Cold sweat broke out on my forehead as it came straight for me. I knew, without doubt, it was carrying a message for me.

I held my hand out, and the butterfly landed on it. A small sound came from it. It was like a whisper. I couldn't make out the words, so I lifted the butterfly to my ear and asked it to repeat the message.

"Cassia!" Gran's voice came from the little creature. "Cassia! Help! Help!" This was followed by Gran screaming.

My knees buckled, and I fell back against my desk. I said to the butterfly, "Where is she? Where's Gran? Is she in Brimstone?"

The butterfly opened its wings and flew away.

My desk phone rang making me jump. I grabbed the receiver. "Gran? Is that you? Are you okay?"

"Ms Winter? It's Doctor Gilbert. I'm at your grandma's house. She's had an accident. Can you come here straightaway?"

Chapter 10

I took a moment to steady myself and to get my heartbeat back to normal. Then I grabbed my bag and dashed out of the office. The sensible part of me made me go over to Cheryl's desk and blurt out, "Cheryl! Family emergency! Have to leave. Appraisals on my desk."

Cheryl took in the severity of the situation immediately and replied, "I'll deal with everything, Cassia. Off you go. I hope everything works out okay."

I raced out of the building and towards the car park. I had no idea I could run so fast. I'm sure I must have broken the speed limit as I jumped in my car and zoomed towards Gran's house. Dr Gilbert didn't give me any details over the phone and said he'd explain everything in person.

I swallowed down the panic as I drove. I couldn't imagine Gran not being in my life. She'd always been there for me. I assumed she always would be.

With a dramatic squeal, I pulled up outside Gran's house, vaguely registered an unfamiliar car outside, and ran into the house.

I found her lying on the sofa in the living room, her head resting against pillows. My heart missed a beat when I saw how pale she was. A man was sitting on a chair at her side with Oliver on his knee.

I knew the man because I'd been to see him many times in the last few months.

Dr Gilbert looked over at me, smiled and said, "Hello there, Cassia. Thanks for coming so quickly. Your Gran here has taken a bit of a tumble. She can't remember yet how it happened."

I went over to Gran's side, dropped to my knees and peered closely at her lovely face. I winced as I saw a purple bruise blooming on her cheek.

I took one of her hands in my own and said, "Gran, what have you been doing? Are you alright? Are you going to the hospital?"

Gran gave me a weak smile and replied, "Stop fussing, I'm fine. I've just been a silly old woman, that's all. I've got a few bruises, but that's it."

Dr Gilbert interjected, "That's not all, she's got a sprained ankle too." He nodded in the direction of Gran's elevated leg, and I saw her left ankle had been bandaged. Dr Gilbert continued, "It's nothing serious, but she does need to rest for a week, maybe two weeks. I've given her some painkillers and some sleeping tablets. They're quite strong and she may nod off soon. Which is a good thing as you know how active your grandma is. She needs lots of rest so she can recover."

My eyes stung as I looked back at Gran. "How did it happen? Were you doing too much again?"

Gran gave me a pointed look and said, "It was nothing, Cassia. Why don't you see Dr Gilbert to the door? I'm sure he's got more important patients to deal with than me."

Dr Gilbert gave Oliver a final stroke on his head before placing him on the ground. He got to his feet and said, "Now, Esther Winter, I'm serious when I say you need to have some rest. You're not as young as you once were, and your healing time will take a lot longer. I'm going to ring Cassia later to see how you're getting on. There's no point phoning you because I know you won't tell me the truth. And there's no need to look at me like that, we've known each other a long time and I know what you're like." He looked in my direction and said, "I'll see myself out. Cassia, are you still coming to see me next week?"

I gave him a brief nod. I was a regular visitor to Dr Gilbert's surgery with my various ailments. I was going to ask him for stronger painkillers for my headaches and to see if he could do anything about my increasingly painful ulcers. But I wasn't going to mention that in front of Gran.

Dr Gilbert said farewell and left the house. As soon as I heard him drive away, I turned my attention back to Gran.

Gran said, "Before you say anything, let me talk first. Those tablets the doctor gave me are already working, and I'm starting to feel drowsy. Cassia, I need to tell you something before I end up in the land of nod."

"Can I just ask if you're feeling okay? Do you need me to get you another pillow? Or a blanket?"

Gran moved her head from side to side, and I noticed her wincing with pain. Oliver jumped on to the sofa and settled himself at Gran's side.

Gran said, "Cassia, I was in Brimstone when I was hurt."

"Brimstone? What happened? Who hurt you?"

"I'll get to the facts a lot quicker if you stop interrupting me. I was working on a case involving Jonathan Tidewell."

"Jonathan Tidewell? Who's he? Is he the one who hurt you?" I rolled up my sleeves. "Tell me where this Jonathan is, I'll soon sort him out."

A ghost of a smile flickered on Gran's face. "Cassia, your resolve is strong, but you wouldn't have been much of a match against Jonathan. He was a werewolf."

I pulled my sleeves back down. "Was a werewolf? What happened to him?"

"I'm trying to get to that point, but you keep interrupting me." Gran let out a little yawn. "Jonathan Tidewell apparently committed suicide by hanging himself from a tree in the forest in Brimstone. The leader of Jonathan's pack, Strom, is concerned about his suicide and thinks something more sinister is at work. Strom was so concerned that he contacted Blythe who then asked me to investigate the matter. So, early this morning I went into the forest to see where the supposed suicide took place."

I shook my head slowly in disbelief. "Gran, are you telling me you went into a forest full of werewolves to see how one of them had died? That can't be safe."

"Cassia, you keep forgetting I'm a witch. Supernatural beings don't mess with me, not if they know what's good for them. Anyway, if you'd let me finish, I went into the forest to examine the tree where Jonathan had killed himself. As I got closer to it, I heard voices; two voices. I walked towards them." Gran frowned. "That's all I can remember. I vaguely recall feeling scared and then running. I think I felt someone pushing me, or shouting at me. And the next thing I knew, I was lying here with Dr Gilbert looking at me with that silly worried expression on his face."

"That doesn't make any sense. How did you get from Brimstone to here? And how did Dr Gilbert know you were injured?"

Gran let out another little yawn before saying, "I don't know how I got back home, but I suspect someone from Brimstone carried me here. That is totally illegal. Residents of Brimstone are not allowed into our world without severe consequences, so whoever brought me here was taking a big risk. I can't think of who would take such a risk unless it was the person who attacked me and they then wanted me out of the way."

"How did Dr Gilbert know about you?"

"I asked him that. He said his receptionist received a phone call about me. The doctor didn't know if it was a male or female who'd phoned. I asked him to ring the receptionist to find out, but she couldn't remember either as they've been so busy this morning. All she could say is that whoever made the call was very curt and said the doctor needed to get here immediately."

Gran settled back on the pillows, and her eyes began to close.

"Gran, what can we do about this? Should I go to Brimstone and find out who attacked you?"

Gran's eyelids flitted open. In a tired voice, she said, "Cassia, leave everything to me. I don't want you getting involved in Brimstone business. I'm sure I'll be up on my feet in no time. If I wasn't so tired and weak, I'd use magic to heal myself."

I swallowed my nervousness before saying, "Could I use some of my magic on you? If you tell me what to do, I could have a go."

The corner of Gran's mouth lifted slowly. "No, thank you. You haven't been trained, and with all the best intentions in the world you might end up turning me into a frog or a caterpillar. No, Cassia, leave everything to me. You get yourself back to work. I'll be fine. And don't even think about going into Brimstone. It's not your concern, and I don't want you to have any part of it. Forget about this magic business and being a witch."

"There's no way I'm going back to the office and leaving you on your own. I'll stay here with you and keep an eye on you."

Gran nodded slowly and her eyelids closed. Within seconds, she was snoring lightly.

I looked at Oliver and raised my eyebrows as if asking him what I should do next. He jumped off the sofa and padded over to the cellar door. I went after him. He must have been thinking the same thing as me.

I looked down at Oliver and said, "I'm going to Brimstone to find out who attacked Gran. Do I need to take anything with me? Some lunch? A coat? Some form of protection which will keep me safe from werewolves?"

Oliver gave me a look as if to say, 'I've no idea; just get on with it.'

I went back over to Gran and made sure she was sound asleep before heading back to the cellar door. I was about to open the door when my phone alerted me to a text. I quickly read it. It was from Alistair, and he was wondering where the hell I was. His words. Anger bubbled up inside me, and my reply was 'Family emergency'. I knew from experience that he would be texting me back within minutes to demand more information. I didn't have time for that. I switched the phone off, put my hand on the cellar door and pulled it open. I ran down the stairs, across the floor and towards the door that would lead me to Brimstone.

I smiled to myself. I hadn't felt this sense of purpose in a long, long time. I was going to find out who attacked my lovely Gran, and if that meant walking into a pack of angry werewolves, so be it.

Chapter 11

I stepped onto the cobbled path, closed the cellar door behind me, and took a moment to take in my surroundings. I could see individuals milling around the town square, busy with their everyday lives. If they knew Gran had been attacked, they showed no obvious signs of it. I glanced towards the butterfly tree at the end of the cobbled path, and saw the butterflies flapping their wings in my direction as if saying hello to me. I realised I'd forgotten to tell Gran about the butterfly who came to my office. Had someone sent it?

I walked closer to the butterflies, raised my hand in greeting and said, "Hi, it's good to see you again. Do any of you know who attacked my gran?" I didn't know what the protocol was for talking to the Brimstone butterflies, but it was worth a try.

The butterflies flapped their wings slowly in return, and I had no idea whether that meant they knew something or not.

"Thanks anyway," I told them, and I walked towards Blythe's house. If anyone knew something about Gran's attack, it would be Blythe.

The door opened before I had the chance to knock on it.

Brin stood there, her brow creased in concern. She said, "We've heard about your gran. How is she? Is she badly hurt? Has she seen a doctor? Is there something I can do to help?"

I quickly explained that Dr Gilbert had seen to her and added, "She's fast asleep on the sofa and her cat, Oliver, is keeping an eye on her, for what that's worth. I'll go back and check on her soon. Is Blythe in? I need to talk to her."

Brin stood to one side. "Of course, come in. She's in the living room. She's in the middle of a meeting, but I'm sure she won't mind you interrupting her."

I walked into the living room and came to a stop when I saw who Blythe was having a meeting with. Fairies of all shapes, sizes and colours filled the room. Some were sitting on the floor, some were perched on furniture, and some were fluttering around the room in an agitated manner.

Blythe noticed me standing by the door and said, "Oh Cassia! We've just heard about Esther. One of the butterflies told us. How is she?"

I repeated my Dr Gilbert conversation to which Blythe replied, "Good, good. Oliver will keep a good eye on her. If she wakes up, he'll let us know."

I blinked. Oliver would let them know? How? Was he going to use a mobile phone or something?

Blythe said, "Don't just stand there, Cassia, come in and take a seat."

I didn't dare move forward; there were fairies everywhere. I said, "I don't want to stand on anyone and squash them."

Blythe looked at the fairies on the carpet in front of me and flapped her hand at them. They quickly made a clear passage for me. I walked along the fairy-free area and took a seat on the sofa, checking for fairies before I lowered my behind.

I began, "Blythe, before Gran fell asleep, she told me about Jonathan Tidewell's suicide."

There was a collective gasp from the fairies, and some of them moved away from me. What was their problem?

Blythe took a seat opposite me and said, "We don't think it was suicide." She nodded in the general direction of the fairies and went on, "We think there's something more sinister afoot. Jonathan was not the kind of werewolf to take his own life. He'd recently got engaged and had every reason to live. Esther was going to make further investigations into his death." Her face brightened up. "Are you here to take on the case on your gran's behalf? That would be incredibly helpful, Cassia."

Without hesitating, I lied, "Yes, that's what Gran wants me to do. She wants me to talk to the leader of the pack and to make a full investigation." It entered my mind that with Blythe being a witch, she might be aware of the lies I was telling her. I put a convincing smile on my face.

Blythe clasped her hands together in delight and let out a big sigh. "That is such a relief. We were thinking of contacting one of the witches from the outer lands to deal with the case. Now we don't have to. What do you need to know from me before you meet the werewolves?"

I forced the smile to stay on my face and tried to give the impression that I wasn't freaked out by the thought of meeting a pack of werewolves. I said, "Where will I find them? Gran mentioned the forest; whereabouts is that?"

Blythe replied, "Some of the fairies here will show you the way. They won't go all the way into the forest, not with the werewolves being the ferocious creatures that they are." She gave a laugh and added, "I'm sure you'll be alright though, Cassia, you're a witch. And the werewolves don't hurt witches. No one in Brimstone hurts witches."

"But someone did hurt Gran," I pointed out. "Can I use magic to defend myself? Is there a wand I could have? Perhaps I could borrow yours."

The fairies let out a shocked gasp as if I'd just suggested running naked down the middle of the street.

Blythe gave me a gentle smile. "Cassia, you don't borrow another witch's wand - ever. Find the leader of the pack, Strom, and get some details about Jonathan and his movements before he died. If you don't upset them, the werewolves will treat you in a fair manner."

I gulped. "But what if they take offence to my gentle questioning? Are you sure there isn't something I can use to defend myself?"

Blythe's purple eyes gave me a deep, searching look. She said, "You already know how to use magic, don't you? You've used witchcraft today with those appraisals of yours."

Sweat broke out on my forehead. "How do you know about that?"

"You performed magic in the human world. I always know when that happens. Don't look so shocked. I'm glad you did use your magical powers. I wish it hadn't been in the human world because you could have been caught, and then goodness knows what might've happened to you." Her searching look intensified. "How did it feel when you performed the magic? How did you set about using it?"

I thought back to the incident. "I felt as if I was focusing my mind on what I wanted to happen. I got a tingle down my hand, and then the magic just happened. It was sort of awesome." I gave her a small grin.

Blythe nodded. "Your intention was good, and your focus was clear. That's exactly how you need to be when you perform magic. I wish I had more time to go through your magical abilities, but I've got something important to deal with. I don't mind telling you, Cassia, there's something strange going on in the lands outside Brimstone. There have been rumours of trouble brewing there for a long time, and I need to meet with the leaders there. Something terrible is heading towards Brimstone, and I have to stop it before any further trouble occurs."

I looked left and right at the fairies and could see their worried expressions mirrored Blythe's.

I said, "More trouble? What do you mean? What's happened?"

Blythe said, "Well, the obvious thing is that Esther has been attacked. Then, she was taken back into your world by someone who lives in Brimstone. That is an unlawful act. Also, there's the matter of Jonathan Tidewell. He didn't commit suicide; he was murdered. We don't have murders often in Brimstone. The last one was a long time ago."

"He was murdered? How do you know?" I asked.

Blythe placed a hand on her stomach. "I can feel it here. And that's where you come in, Cassia. You're going to make a full investigation and find out who murdered Jonathan."

A fairy flew over to her and whispered something in her ear.

Blythe got to her feet, and said to me, "We have to leave now. Something is happening in the outer lands. Cassia, I wish I could offer you more help, but I'm afraid I'll have to leave this murder investigation up to you. Will you be able to deal with it?"

Mustering all the determination and courage I could, I stood up, gave Blythe a confident smile and said, "Of course I can deal with the murder of a werewolf."

Chapter 12

A purple fairy the size of my hand flew over to my ear, and said, "We'll show you the way to the forest. Follow me."

Blythe said, "Cassia, are you sure you can handle this? We can always ask someone else to deal with it."

I gave her a manic smile. "I can deal with this, no problem. I've watched Teen Wolf. I know what to expect from werewolves. And I've watched all the Twilight films." I gave her a nod as if to confirm I was a werewolf expert.

Blythe's brow furrowed. "Teen Wolf? Twilight? I've heard of those, but they're not based on facts. Cassia, I'm having second thoughts about this."

I lifted my chin and walked confidently towards the door. Without giving Blythe another glance, I said, "I'm only going to talk to the werewolves. I'm sure I won't be in danger. Cheerio!"

I managed to keep hold of my courage as I was followed out of Blythe's home by a group of purple fairies. We stepped out of the front door and turned right. One fairy flew near my left ear, and another by my right. I looked over my shoulder and saw the other four fairies were flying behind me in pairs. My heart skipped a beat as I realised they looked like a funeral procession with me as the coffin. I shook my head. I could do without thoughts like that.

We walked down a path at the side of the house and towards a wooden gate. I pushed the gate open and stepped onto a stone path which was lined with pebbles.

The lead fairy said, "This way."

I did as I was told and walked along the stone path for about five minutes. There were trees either side of the path and the sun shone through the leaves. Birds tweeted, and small butterflies fluttered in and out of the trees. It was all very pleasant, and I felt my spirits lifting. Maybe talking to werewolves wouldn't be that bad after all.

The stone path ended, and the fairies hovered silently in the air.

The lead fairy said, "This is where we leave you."

I looked in front of me and noticed four separate dirt paths going in different directions. None of them looked welcoming.

I said to the fairy, "Which way do I go now? And why can't you come with me?"

She replied, "It's not safe for us to go further into the forest." She hesitated and then added, "I'm sure you'll be alright. You are a witch after all. Follow the path on the furthest left. It will take you to where the werewolves live." There was another hesitation before she said, "Good luck."

The fairies flew away in the blink of an eye, and I found myself all alone on the path.

I mumbled to myself, "Come on, Cassia, you can do this. You're only going for a little chat. So, you're going to talk to werewolves! Big deal. You can handle this."

I turned to the furthest path on the left and stepped on to it. I forced myself forward. My heartbeat was going much, much faster than my reluctant legs. As I walked further along, the trees became denser and the birdsong stopped. There wasn't one single happy butterfly fluttering about anywhere.

Gulping down my fear, I continued walking. I nearly jumped out of my skin when I heard the snap of a twig to my right. I glanced nervously that way, but couldn't see anything other than dense foliage. Was someone watching me?

My steps were even slower as I moved forward. A sudden rustling of leaves made me jump again. I heard a snort of something, or someone, to my left and my head turned that way. I had the uneasy feeling that someone was watching every step that I was taking.

At this point, I did what any sensible person who's watched horror movies would do - I turned around and retreated down the path.

I'd only gone a few steps when I came to a stop and said to myself, "Come on Cassia! Don't be a wimp. Don't forget about Gran. Someone hurt her. No one messes with Gran. You can do this. You are a witch." I raised my fist in the air and waved it at the trees around me. "Don't mess with me."

I lifted my chin, turned around on the spot and marched back along the path at a more determined pace. Thankfully, my determination stayed with me all the way along the ever-darkening path.

I soon came to a clearing. In the middle of the clearing were about a dozen wooden cabins with smoke coming out of their chimneys. A collection of wooden cabins sounds quite comforting, but it was the grim-faced men who stood in a line in front of the biggest cabin that ruined the friendly scene for me.

The men were all thickset with huge muscles rippling beneath their shirts and jeans. They were watching me with eyes full of suspicion. Were these the werewolves I was looking for? Or just a group of angry-looking men trying to live a quiet life?

One of the men lifted his head and inhaled noisily. His eyes glittered, and he licked his lips. He smiled, showing protruding canine teeth.

So, they were werewolves then. Had they eaten recently? Was I going to be their lunch? There were about ten or twelve men glowering at me, and I was certain I wasn't big enough to go around all of them. That thought didn't give me the slightest bit of reassurance.

The biggest man stepped forward and gave me the once over. It was clear he was older than the rest by the flecks of grey in his hair, his craggy-looking face and the wrinkles at the corners of his eyes. He had various claw-shaped scars down both cheeks which led me to surmise he'd been in many fights.

I attempted a smile and said in a pathetically feeble voice, "Hello. Sorry to disturb you. I'm – "

The man spoke, "Cassia Winter. We know who you are. I'm Strom, the leader of this pack." He came closer and held out his hand. It was the size of a shovel. As I placed my impossibly small hand in his he continued, "We've heard about your gran. How is Esther?"

"She's fine, thank you. She's a bit bruised and has a sprained ankle, but she's going to recover." I wasn't sure why I was going into so much detail as it could have been this werewolf who attacked Gran. I quickly retrieved my hand.

Strom said, "I've known Esther a long time, and I hope she recovers quickly. We know why you're here, and we thank you for coming. You're here to talk about Jonathan Tidewell."

A man suddenly broke forward and yelled, "Don't talk to her! She's of no use to us. She's weak willed and lacks courage. I can smell it on her. Tell her to go! This is werewolf business; we can deal with this ourselves. We don't need outsiders here, especially not someone like her."

Strom bared his teeth at the man who had just spoken and growled, "Flint! That's enough. I'm dealing with this. Get back to your work." He looked at the other men who were still giving me dark looks, and ordered, "The rest of you can get back to work too. I'm dealing with this."

There was a bit of grumbling, but one by one, the other men turned away and headed towards their cabins. The one called Flint gave me a particularly evil look before turning away.

Strom indicated his big hand towards a table and said, "Take a seat, and we'll talk about Jonathan. Is there anything I can do for Esther? Do you know who attacked her?"

"I was about to ask you the same thing." I couldn't keep the accusing tone from my voice.

Strom's thick eyebrows rose. "Do you think one of us attacked her? I know we werewolves have a rough reputation, but I don't think for a minute any member of my pack would do that to Esther. And they certainly wouldn't have carried her back to the human world. They know that's illegal. However, I can assure you that if someone here is responsible for the attack, not only will they have to deal with Blythe, they'll have to deal with me too."

I took a seat and glanced towards the log cabin where Flint was standing. He had his eyes on me, and I tried not to shiver at the hate that was aimed my way.

Strom took a seat opposite me and laid his hands on the table. He said, "Let me tell you more about Jonathan, and then you can ask me about anything I've missed out. Let me start by asking how much you know about werewolves."

I shrugged. A light-hearted quip about *Teen Wolf* and *Twilight* didn't seem appropriate here, and I had a feeling Strom would be insulted if I mentioned them. He might not be aware of what they were, but I didn't want to take that chance.

Strom continued, "There are different kinds of werewolves. Some are born as werewolves like myself and most of my pack, but some are humans who have been bitten. Jonathan was the latter kind." He shook his head sorrowfully. "It's my fault that Jonathan was bitten and turned into a werewolf. It was one of my pack who bit him."

"Was it Flint?"

Strom gave me a half smile. "No, it wasn't Flint, although he is quick to anger. No, it was a rogue wolf who I was having problems with. I won't trouble you with the details, but he was trying to take over my leadership amongst other things. We argued, and he left the pack. It was for the best, or so I thought. Then I heard he'd entered the human world and attacked Jonathan. He killed Jonathan's wife and son. I had no option but to go into your world and find Jonathan before he fully turned into a werewolf. I couldn't have him doing that in front of humans. He wouldn't be able to control himself."

My TV werewolf information came to the front of my mind, and I said, "Would he have turned into a werewolf after killing something? Or am I thinking of vampires?"

A glint of amusement came into Strom's eyes. "Something like that. But I was too late. Jonathan had completed his werewolf transformation by the time I got to him, and he was running wild. I couldn't leave him in the human world. I brought him here and adopted him into our clan."

"What happened to the rogue werewolf?" I asked.

Strom looked down at his hands and flexed his big fingers. "I ended his life. I had to." He looked back at me. "Jonathan was in shock for weeks, as you can imagine, and we had many talks together. He was a sensible man, and he did his best to come to terms with his new condition. He was of strong character, and it didn't take him long to join in with the rest of the pack. He was a hard worker, and naturally of a happy disposition. He made the best of his new situation and even made plans for the future. He had no reason to take his own life; he had everything to live for. He'd even recently got engaged to be married."

"Who to?"

Strom lifted his chin proudly and said, "My one and only daughter, Anju. They were perfect together. The addition of Jonathan to our family was going to make it even stronger."

I asked, "How is your daughter coping with Jonathan's death?"

Strom shook his head sadly. "She's devastated. She hasn't spoken to anyone for days."

"Did Jonathan have any enemies?"

"Yes, Flint. He was betrothed to Anju last year, but she ended it. I'm not entirely sure why, but I think it was something to do with his controlling ways."

My attention went over to Flint who was still watching me. I made a mental note -Flint is suspect number one.

I said to Strom, "Can I see where the incident took place, please? If that's not too disrespectful."

Strom got to his feet and pointed to a small path at the side of us. "Follow that path until you come to a clearing with a huge oak tree in the middle. You can't miss it." He paused a moment before continuing, "Take care out there. I can control my pack, up to a point, but there are other creatures in this forest who you wouldn't want to meet."

Chapter 13

I said goodbye to Strom and then headed down the narrow path. I tried my best to ignore the twig cracking noises that accompanied my walk. I was getting annoyed with whoever was trying to scare me.

I continued down the path and came to the opening where a majestic oak tree stood. I tilted my head. I could hear someone crying. I focused my attention on the base of the tree and spotted someone small curled up against it.

The sobbing suddenly increased. I couldn't help myself. I ran over to the crying creature and enquired, "Are you alright? Well, obviously, you're not alright. Sorry, that was a stupid question."

The creature turned around and looked up at me. She was dressed in brown clothes and had short, spiky brown hair. Her big eyes were green, and her ears were pointed. An elf? She picked herself up from her kneeling position and wiped dirt from her brown trousers. She only came up to my waist.

"I'm sorry, I didn't mean to disturb you," I said. I dug into my pocket and retrieved a tissue. Thankfully, it was a clean tissue. I held it towards her.

She took the tissue and gave me a wobbly smile. "It's me who should be apologising for crying, and out in the open like this. I'm Tansy; I'm a forest elf. I know who you are. You're Cassia Winter. I heard about your gran. How is she?"

Everyone in Brimstone seemed to know Gran had been attacked, but no one knew who had done it. Suspicious? I thought so. Was there a conspiracy going on?

I looked down at the elf and said, "Gran is going to be fine. Thank you for asking. Why were you crying? Is it something to do with Jonathan Tidewell? Did you know him?"

Tansy broke into a fresh stream of sobs, and I waited until she composed herself. I felt like I should be patting her back and saying soothing words, but I wasn't sure how you should comfort an elf seeing as I'd never met one before. What was elf etiquette? That's something I'd have to discuss with Blythe later. She was going to be my Brimstone equivalent of Google.

Once Tansy had composed herself and wiped her tears away, she said, "I did know Jonathan. He did work for me. He did a lot of work for many elves and creatures in this forest."

"What sort of work?"

"He helped with general house repairs and gardening work for those who struggled. He replaced some tiles on my roof a while ago, and he cleared my gutters out. He was so helpful and so good-natured. Not like the other werewolves at all. We shall miss him greatly around here."

I said, "Can you tell me more about Jonathan, and how he dealt with being a werewolf?"

"He dealt well with what he called his curse," Tansy replied. "He didn't talk about it often, and there were certain times during the month when he couldn't do work for me because of the full moon. He seemed to resent having to take time away from his work." She flinched and looked towards the trees behind us. "Did you hear that? I thought I heard something moving over there."

I looked at the trees and frowned in their direction. Whoever was following me, if someone was, was really getting on my nerves now.

I said to Tansy, "I don't know much about werewolves. What happened when Jonathan was affected by the full moon? Did he lose control of himself?"

"He went into a steel cage for the duration of his change. His pack leader, Strom had built him a strong steel cage with extra locks at Jonathan's request. Jonathan accepted he would change during the full moon, but he wanted to do it in a safe environment where he wouldn't be a danger to anyone."

"Does that happen with all the other werewolves too?"

Tansy frowned. "No, they're different to Jonathan. Most of them were born as werewolves, and as they grew up, they were taught how to change into wolves at will rather than relying on the moon. They were also taught to control themselves during a transformation and to be aware of what they're doing. But Jonathan didn't want to go through the training that was offered to him. He spoke to me now and again about it, and said he wanted to remain as human as he possibly could." She frowned again and added, "Despite his happy ways, I don't think Jonathan was happy being a werewolf, not at first anyway."

"I've just spoken to Strom, and he told me Jonathan was making a new life for himself. He mentioned Jonathan had recently become engaged to his daughter."

Tansy smiled. "Anju. Yes, she's an exception. She's not like the other werewolves. She's lovely and always has a kind word for us elves. Not like some. Jonathan told me about the engagement, and I was so happy for him. It sounded as if he was finally accepting his werewolf life. I thought he was going to find some peace." She looked towards the trees again. "Are you sure you can't hear that sound? I keep hearing someone moving over there."

"I can't hear anything. Can you tell me more about Jonathan's engagement?"

Tansy said, "Yes, of course. I thought he would be happy and was accepting himself as a werewolf. But he wasn't. A few days after telling me about the engagement, I noticed a change in him. He wasn't as happy as he normally was, and there was a restlessness about him. Also, he wasn't sleeping well, and I suspected something was bothering him. Whatever it was, he wouldn't talk to me about it."

I looked at the oak tree in front of us and said, "When did you last see Jonathan?"

Tansy looked up at the tree too. "He came to do some gardening work for me a few days before he died. That was the last time I saw him, but I did hear him having an argument with someone on the morning he died."

"An argument? Who with?" I looked down at the elf who was now twisting the bottom of her shirt in agitation.

Tansy lowered her voice, and an anxious look came into her eyes. "He was arguing with another werewolf called Flint."

"I've met Flint. What were they arguing about?"

Tansy swallowed nervously and said, "I shouldn't be talking about this. I'm sure I can feel someone listening to us."

"Tansy, this is important. I need to know about Jonathan's last days."

Tansy beckoned me to lower my head, which I did. She whispered in my ear, "They were arguing about Anju. Flint was yelling at Jonathan and saying he wasn't good enough for her, and that he wasn't even a proper werewolf. He told Jonathan to go back to the human world where he belonged. Jonathan shouted back that he was worthy of Anju's love, and that they were going to be happy together. He said Flint was only jealous, and that he should deal with it. They kept arguing back and forth. I was in my garden at the time and their voices were coming from the forest nearby. I didn't like hearing Jonathan so angry. I've never heard him shout like that before. I turned around and went back inside my house."

I didn't want to ask the next question, but I had to. "Do you think Flint killed Jonathan and then made it look like suicide?"

Tansy quickly nodded. She put her little hands on my head and pulled me even closer. She whispered, "Not only was Flint jealous about Jonathan marrying Anju, he was jealous about Jonathan becoming the alpha male. Strom was going to stand down as the alpha male once Jonathan and Anju married. Flint couldn't bear the thought of that. He thought he was the best one for that role." She released my head and gave me a knowing look.

I said to her, "Would Strom have been happy about standing down as pack leader?"

Tansy frowned. "I think so. Jonathan didn't talk about it much." She suddenly clutched my leg and hissed, "Someone is listening! They've heard everything I've said to you! They'll be after me next."

I looked at the trembling elf and felt guilty about causing her distress. That didn't stop me from asking another question. "Tansy, is there anything else you can tell me about Jonathan? Anything important about his last days?"

She began to shake even more, and her eyes were fixed on the trees behind us. She hissed, "I can feel them watching us. I'm scared." She turned terrified eyes in my direction. "I have to go. I can't talk to you anymore."

"Do you want me to come with you?" I wasn't sure what use I would be against whoever was watching us, but I could try.

Tansy shook her head. Her eyes brimmed with tears. "Cassia, be careful. I think someone did kill Jonathan and they're trying to cover it up. Take care of yourself." She gave me a brief smile before turning and running away.

I watched her go, and then looked up at the oak tree again. There was one branch which was thicker than the others, and I noticed a couple of marks on it. Rope marks?

If someone did kill Jonathan, who was it and what was their motive? Flint was the obvious one. But what about Strom? Did he really want to give up being the alpha male?

I needed to talk to other people about the werewolves, and their relationships with each other. My thoughts went to Gran. I wanted to go back to her house and check on her. Had Gran uncovered something important during her short investigation? Had the killer seen her near this crime scene?

I took one final look at the oak tree and then turned around and headed back towards the path which had brought me here. There was rustling behind me and more cracking of twigs. I pressed my lips together and could feel my nostrils flaring in annoyance. Whoever was trying to scare me was doing a terrible job.

Or so I told myself. As I walked quickly along the path, I could hear soft footsteps behind me. My steps speeded up, and so did my breathing. I didn't dare look behind me. I broke into a jog. It turned into a full sprint when I heard someone breathing heavily behind me.

My legs pounded down the path, and my arms pumped furiously at my side in an effort to make me run faster. I heard a soft laugh behind me, but it wasn't a joyful kind of laugh. It was the kind of laugh that says 'I'm coming to get you and there's nothing you can do to stop me.'

My legs went even faster, and I could see the end of the path. I ran towards it, but I was suddenly grabbed and pulled into the trees.

Chapter 14

I rolled over several times in the undergrowth before coming to a stop. It took me a moment to get my eyes to focus, and when I did, I found myself looking into the deep blue eyes of a rabbit. The rabbit's nose twitched, and it placed its little furry paw on my arm.

"Hello, Mr Rabbit. Did you see who pulled me off the path?" I pulled myself into a sitting position and looked left and right. "I bet it was that werewolf, Flint. I bet he's the one who's been following me and listening to my conversation with Tansy." I looked back at the rabbit and gave him a smile. "I don't know why I'm talking to you. It's not like you can answer me or anything."

The rabbit continued to stare at me with those deep blue eyes. Deep blue eyes? Did rabbits have deep blue eyes? I had no idea, but I suspected they didn't. There was only one person I'd met with that shade of blue in his eyes. But he hadn't been a rabbit. What was going on here?

Feeling ridiculous, I gently touched the rabbit's paw and whispered, "Luca? Is that you?"

I quickly removed my hand and shook my head at my foolishness. I must have bumped my head on something as I rolled through the undergrowth.

What happened next confirmed something must have happened to my brain during my tumble. The rabbit immediately began to grow and then it stood upright on its back legs. I rubbed my eyes as the rabbit turned into Luca. I'd have to make an appointment with the doctor as soon as I returned home. I would need a brain scan. I was totally imagining things now.

Luca spoke. I rubbed my ears. Not only was I imagining strange things, I was also hearing things too.

I held my hands palms up to Luca and said, "You're an illusion. A mirage. Go away. I don't have time for this."

Luca threw his head back and laughed. When he looked back at me, he said, "Cassia, have you forgotten what I am?"

I shook my head wildly. "Can you please stop talking? Mirages don't talk. I'm trying to clear my head."

Luca moved closer to me and nipped my arm. It wasn't imaginary pain that shot through me; it was real pain.

"Ouch!" I rubbed my arm. "What did you do that for?"

Luca grabbed my hands and pulled me to my feet. His hands felt very real and solid in mine and I held on to them.

He gazed into my eyes with those amazing blue eyes and I felt myself going dizzy.

He said, "Cassia, don't you remember anything about me at all? Don't you remember all the fun times we had together when we were children?"

I took my hands from his and my head immediately cleared. "Luca, I've only recently started to remember things from my past. Were you a rabbit just now? No, you can't have been. That's ridiculous."

Luca gave me a kind smile. "Of course I was just a rabbit. I am a shapeshifter. You must remember that Cassia, surely?"

A little snort erupted from me. "A shapeshifter? Really? A proper shapeshifter who shifts into different shapes? That's absurd."

Luca opened his arms wide and said, "Don't forget where you are. You're in a magical country now where supernatural creatures abound. Cassia, think clearly. Try to remember. Please." There was a pleading tone in his voice which I couldn't resist.

I concentrated on his face for a while, and a flash of a memory came to me. I was running in a field full of daisies, and there was a rabbit by my side. I looked down at the rabbit, and I knew immediately it was Luca. Just as quickly, the memory disappeared.

I frowned. "A shapeshifter? If you're a shapeshifter, why would you turn into a rabbit? Why not turn into a dragon or a dinosaur or a – " I stopped myself as I realised I was talking nonsense.

Luca said, "My preferred shape is a rabbit because that was your favourite animal when you were young. I can turn into other small animals too. And, when the situation needs it, I can turn into something more ferocious. But that's not something I like to do. There are many rabbits and small creatures in this forest and around Brimstone, and being small allows me to blend in with them."

"Why would you want to blend in with them?"

"Because of my job as a guardian. Blending in is perfect when I'm working in the forest. I like to take on a small shape so that I can go about my work unnoticed."

I scrunched my face up in confusion. "Guardian? Guardian of what? Luca, you'll have to explain everything to me. I've had a very confusing day, in fact, I've had a couple of very confusing days."

Luca put his hand on my arm and led me over to a rock. He sat down and indicated for me to do the same. I did so and turned my face towards him.

He began, "We don't have a police force here in Brimstone. I think you have a police force in the human world, is that right? Your gran explained it to me once, and it sounded very complicated."

"Yes, we do have a police force. If you don't have that here, what system do you have to make sure laws are enforced?"

"We have the guardians. Like myself. We're mainly shapeshifters which allows us to change into our animal selves and then patrol the town discreetly. We keep an eye on everyone and make sure no one is breaking the law. If someone does something unlawful, we immediately report back to Blythe. The residents of Brimstone know we patrol the town, but they're never really sure if the rabbit or mouse they see scampering around the town square is a guardian or not. It's amazing how the residents of Brimstone behave themselves if they think they're being watched."

My eyebrows rose. "So, you're like CCTV? But with rabbits?"

"CCTV? I don't know what that is."

I looked towards the trees and thought about Luca's job as a guardian. I said to him, "If you're watching people all the time, does that mean you go into their homes and watch them there? That seems rather intrusive. Don't you have privacy laws here?"

"We only patrol the public areas. What people do behind closed doors is their own business, unless it is something unlawful. That's where your gran helps out. If a crime is committed, your gran is made aware of it, and she makes the appropriate investigations. The guardians and witches work well together. There's never been a problem, so far." He tapped me on the shoulder so that I turned to face him. "Which brings me to my next question. What are you doing out here on your own? It's a dangerous place, and there are werewolves everywhere. There was one following you along the path just now which is why I pulled you out of the way."

"Who was it? Who was the werewolf who was following me?"

"You won't know him, he's called Flint. He's a nasty werewolf with a quick temper. He's gone on his way now. I don't know why he was in his wolf form, and why he was following you. Cassia, you haven't answered my question. What are you doing out here?"

"I'm investigating the death of Jonathan Tidewell. And I do know who Flint is. I met him when I spoke to Strom a short while ago."

Luca put his hands up to halt my explanation. "Stop right there. Start at the beginning. What are you talking about? You're investigating the death of Jonathan Tidewell? That's not something you should be doing. That's your gran's job."

"Haven't you heard? Gran was investigating this case when she was attacked."

The colour faded from Luca's face. "She was attacked? Who by? When? Is she alright? Who did it?"

I held my hands up now to halt his questions. "She was attacked when she was in Brimstone, but she can't remember much about it. She's okay, and she's back home. She told me about Jonathan's case. That's why I'm here. I'm investigating it on Gran's behalf. I'm in this area because I've been talking to the werewolves."

Luca shook his head. "You shouldn't be doing this. You're not experienced. You don't have the knowledge required to be investigating the case. You should leave it to someone else. I could even investigate the case. I've worked with your gran before. I know what I'm doing. Leave everything to me, Cassia. It's not safe out here for someone like you."

Anger flashed through me. Just like Alistair had done before, Luca was attempting to tell me what to do. What was it with these men? Why did they think they knew what was best for me?

I jabbed a finger at his chest. "I know how to deal with a murder investigation. I've watched hundreds of detective shows with Gran. Murder, She wrote, Poirot, Miss Marple, Midsomer Murders. I know the procedure. You interview everyone who knew the victim, and then you find out more about the victim's life. Don't tell me what to do when it comes to murder investigations."

Luca's brow creased. "I've no idea what you're talking about. Cassia, this is a dangerous place. You don't know how to protect yourself. You don't even remember how to do magic."

"Remember how to do magic? What do you mean by that? Have I done magic before that you know of?" I kept the appraisal magic to myself. He didn't need to know about that.

Luca broke into a grin, and the charming dimples appeared in his cheeks. My anger diminished a little. He really did have a lovely face.

Luca said, "You used to do magic when you were little. Do you remember when you'd chase me through the fields when I was a rabbit?"

"Vaguely."

"You'd wave your hands around and make the daisies in the field lift up and fly through the air."

"Did I?"

Luca nodded. "You used to talk to trees too. Don't you remember that?"

"Talk to trees? That's a ridiculous thing to do." I paused and remembered where I was. "Did they talk back?"

Luca laughed. "No, but you said you could feel what they were feeling." His smile faded. "Cassia, can't you remember anything? We were such good friends, and we had some wonderful times together. I know we were only young, but I remember everything. Why did you stop coming to Brimstone? What happened when you were seven? I waited by your cellar door every day for months, but you never came through."

I lowered my head. I'd been sitting on the other side of the cellar door waiting for Mum to come back.

I got to my feet and said, "Well, I must be going. I've got a murder investigation to deal with."

Luca stood up. "You're so stubborn. If you insist on going ahead with this investigation, then I'm going to help you."

"No, you're not. I can do this on my own."

"But – "

"No!" I said rather too loudly. "This is something I need to do on my own. I don't need your help." I looked at a couple of dirt paths in front of me. I had no idea which one would lead me back to Brimstone. Keeping my eyes away from Luca, I said, "Could you kindly tell me which path I should take?"

There was an amused tone in Luca's voice as he said, "I thought you didn't need my help."

"Fine. I'll find my own way back." I set off towards the left dirt path.

There was a polite cough behind me, and Luca said, "If you're heading back to the town square, you need to go on the path on the right-hand side."

"Fine," I said again. I changed direction and stepped towards the path on the right-hand side. Remembering my manners, I called over my shoulder, "Thank you."

Chapter 15

As I walked along the path, my anger towards Luca faded. Those childhood memories started coming back to me, and I remembered what good friends Luca and I had been. He was only being helpful by offering his assistance. It wasn't his fault that I had anger issues with Alistair. I would apologise to Luca later.

It didn't take me long to reach the town square, and my attention was immediately drawn towards the gazebo. Flint was standing there in his human form. His eyes were on me as I made my way through the town. What was his problem? Why had he been following me? And why had he been in wolf form when he was doing it? Did he want to hurt me?

I averted my gaze and carried on walking. I headed towards Blythe's house, and as I did a niggling feeling dropped into my brain. I quickly scanned the town square. There was something different about it, but I couldn't quite put my finger on what that was.

I walked up the sparkling path to Blythe's front door and knocked on it sharply. I glanced over my shoulder to make sure no angry werewolf was following me. The path behind me was clear.

Brin answered the door and looked up at me.

"Hello, Brin," I began. "Is Blythe in?"

The little house Brownie shook her head. "No, I'm sorry. She's been called out to a meeting in the outer lands. How did your talk go with the werewolves? I hope they didn't frighten you."

"I'm still in one piece. Just about. Do you know when Blythe will be back?"

Anguish crossed Brin's features. "I don't. I'm not sure how long her meeting will go on. She's talking with other witches." She shook her head. "I shouldn't be telling you this, but I'm worried about the changes that are going on in this town."

"What sort of changes?"

Brin forced a smile to her face, and said, "Sorry, I shouldn't have said anything. I'll let Blythe know that you called and that you returned in one piece from the werewolves. Oh! I nearly forgot. Blythe asked me to pass this to your gran."

She dug her hand into her pocket and retrieved a small glass bottle which had a purple liquid in it. She handed it to me and explained, "It's a levitation potion for Esther. She only needs to take a few drops. Blythe knows it's impossible for Esther to take bed rest while she's recovering, so a few drops of this will levitate her off the ground. Then she won't put any pressure on her sprained ankle."

I took the bottle and put it in my pocket. "That's very thoughtful of Blythe. Please, say thank you to her from me."

Brin nodded. "Where are you going now? You're welcome to come in and have some food with me."

"No, thank you. I want to get back to Gran and make sure she's okay. I'll come back soon."

Brin gave me an intense look. "You take care, Cassia Winter. I'll let Blythe know you called."

She flashed me a smile and closed the door. I turned around and walked back along the brick path.

As I headed along the street I kept my eyes firmly averted from the gazebo. I knew Flint was still staring at me because I could feel the hate coming towards me in waves.

I turned right at the end of the road and was thankful to see the cobbled road which led to Gran's cellar door. I headed towards it, and that's when I realised what was wrong.

I stopped near the butterfly tree and looked at it in horror. The Brimstone butterflies had gone. Every single one of them. All that was left were bare branches. I turned around and looked at the other butterfly trees dotted around the town square. They were bare too. Where had the butterflies gone? Were they all working at the same time? Had there been a sudden run on messages for the butterflies to deliver?

I recalled what Luca had told me about talking to trees and picking up on its feelings. Could I still do that? It was worth a go.

I moved closer to the tree in front of me and placed my hands on its trunk. A slight vibration travelled into my fingers, and I closed my eyes. I knew I probably looked like a nincompoop standing there, but I didn't care. I had to do this. I had to find out where the butterflies had gone.

The first feeling that came to me was the same niggling worry I'd had when I first came into the town square. Something was wrong, but I couldn't work out what it was. Another feeling arrived. It made my stomach clench with unease, and I knew instinctively the butterflies were not out delivering messages. Something was definitely wrong here. That feeling was quickly replaced by one of terror. My heartbeat thudded loudly in my ears, and a chill ran down my back. Something horrific had happened!

I took my hands off the tree and tried to make sense of those feelings. The Brimstone butterflies were terrified about something. But what? And where had they gone? I wished Blythe was still here so I could talk to her about it. Perhaps Gran could help.

Without hesitation, I rushed down the cobbled path and opened the cellar door at the end. I went through and closed the door behind me. The thought of Flint coming through entered my mind, and I looked desperately for a lock on the door. There wasn't one! Why wasn't there one? There should be one.

Someone from Brimstone had brought Gran through in her unconscious state, and what was to stop someone else from coming through now?

I looked towards the table that I used to sit at and went over to it. I dragged it across the floor and placed it in front of the door. I wasn't sure what use it would be as it was only a child's table. Still, it was something. If someone did come through the cellar door, perhaps the table would make a scraping noise which would alert me to the intruder's presence. It wasn't perfect, but it would have to do for now.

I dashed across the cellar and raced up the stairs. I found Gran still asleep on the sofa in the living room with Oliver sitting on the carpet at her side. I went over to Gran's side and knelt next to Oliver.

Her eyelids fluttered open, and she looked in my direction. She gave me a tired smile and said, "Cassia, where did you come from? Where have you been?"

I decided it was time to tell Gran the truth. "I've been to Brimstone, Gran."

Gran gently nodded her head. "Brimstone. That's nice."

I continued, "I've been looking into Jonathan's murder investigation. I've been talking to the werewolves."

Gran nodded again, and her eyelids drooped. "Murder. That's nice. Werewolves. How lovely."

It was obvious Gran was still out of it. How strong were those tablets the doctor had given her? There was no point asking her anything about Jonathan and the rest of his pack at this stage. I'd have to wait until Gran was more awake.

"Gran, let me get you upstairs and into your bed. You can't be very comfortable on the sofa."

Gran gave me a tired smile. "My bed. That would be nice."

"I've got a levitating potion from Blythe. I'm not sure how it works." I took the bottle from my pocket and unscrewed the top. The end bit was like a pipette, so I drew up a small amount of purple liquid from the bottle and then asked Gran to open her mouth. She did so willingly, and I put a few drops of the purple liquid on it.

Before I'd even finished putting the top back on the bottle, Gran was hovering above the sofa.

She chuckled and said, "I must be flying. Look, I'm flying." She rose even more.

I got to my feet and took hold of one of Gran's hands and pulled her towards the stairs. It was like holding on to a balloon, albeit a chuckling Gran-shaped balloon in a cardigan. Gran floated happily at my side as I manoeuvred her up the stairs and towards her bedroom. I made sure I didn't bang her head on the way.

Once in her bedroom, I aimed her towards the bed, pulled the covers back and put her into position above the bed.

"Now what?" I asked myself as I let go of Gran's hand. She rose slightly in the air. I couldn't leave her floating about like this. She might float away into the bathroom and hurt herself. Perhaps it was time to try out my magic skills again.

I opened my hands towards Gran and thought about lowering her to the bed. My hands tingled, and a second later Gran gently floated down to her bed. I quickly pulled the covers over her. I located some heavy books and used them to act as paperweights at the corners of the bed. Once the last makeshift paperweight was in place, I stood back and surveyed my work.

"That should keep you in place, Gran." I sighed heavily. "Now, what am I supposed to do about this murder investigation?"

A male voice behind me said, "You can talk to me about it."

Chapter 16

I picked up one of the book paperweights, spun around and raised it. I yelled, "Don't even think about attacking me! I've got a book, and I'm not afraid to use it!"

I scanned the room. There wasn't anyone there. Well, not anyone that I could see. Ah! There was probably some malicious evil creature in front of me who had turned themselves invisible. They'd most likely sneaked through the cellar door with me and had been in the house watching my every move.

I raised the book even higher and declared, "Show yourself, you coward."

There was no response. I looked at the carpet and saw Oliver sitting there, watching me with his green eyes.

"Oliver, quick! Come over here. There's some sort of invisible creature in the room, and they're here to get us. Come over here, and I'll keep you safe."

Was it my imagination or did Oliver just roll his eyes?

The male voice spoke again, "It's me. I'm the one who spoke to you. Put the book down."

My eyes darted left and right. Where was the hideous creature lurking? "Oliver!" I hissed. "Get to my side quickly. Did you hear that? Did you hear that nasty voice then? We're under attack by an invisible force."

"Cassia, it's me who's speaking. Me, Oliver, the cat. Stop waving that book around and look down at me. You can see my jaw moving."

I stiffened and slowly turned my head in Oliver's direction. "Pardon? Did you make a noise then?"

Oliver actually tutted, and he did roll his eyes, I saw it clear as day. His little jaw opened, and he said, "Cassia, I can talk. I'm a talking cat. Get over it. And put that book down before you drop it on yourself."

I lowered the book and continued to stare at Oliver. "But how? A talking cat? That's impossible."

Oliver padded closer to me. "A talking cat is impossible? Really? Think about what you've seen and heard over the last few days. You've been to a magical land where supernatural creatures walk about free and easy. According to what you told Esther downstairs, you've spoken to werewolves today. And you've finally realised you're a witch. You think a talking cat is out of the realms of possibility? Really? Cassia, pull yourself together."

Without taking my eyes off Oliver, I slowly put the book back down on Gran's bed cover. "You can really talk? How long have you been talking?"

"All my life. Next question."

"Does Gran know you can talk?"

"Of course, we have many conversations. Also, I help her with her investigations in Brimstone. Next question."

I narrowed my eyes at him. "I've lived with Gran for most of my life, and I've never heard you talk. Why is that?"

Oliver gave me a look as if to say it was obvious. He said, "You've only just remembered you're a witch. It would have scared the living daylights out of you if I'd have spoken to you before you came to your witch senses. Esther told me not to anyway. Although, I was tempted to many times when you were growing up. You could have done with some feline advice many times. Have you got any more questions or can we go downstairs and discuss this murder case? I've met the werewolves, and I've got a thing or two to say about them." He lifted his tail in the air, turned around and stalked out of the room.

I nodded my head slowly as I watched him leave. A talking cat. Of course he would be a talking cat. That's what Blythe must've meant when she said Oliver would let her know if anything was wrong with Gran. Of course. I kept nodding to myself as if hoping that would make the information easier to accept.

I looked over at Gran to see how she was doing. She was still snoring gently, and it looked as if she would be that way for a while yet.

I tucked the blanket more firmly around her shoulders and muttered, "Well, I suppose I'd better go downstairs and speak to the talking cat. Yep, a talking cat."

When I got downstairs, Oliver was settled on the sofa. He looked over at me and said, "Get yourself a strong cup of tea. And a chocolate biscuit for the shock of hearing me talk for the first time. Then we can have a chat."

I could only nod. It was beyond weird that he was now talking to me. I took my time as I made myself a cup of tea. It wasn't that hard to believe, was it? I'd seen a shapeshifter today along with many fairies, and, of course, those werewolves. But, still, a talking cat? That would take some getting used to.

I took my tea and two biscuits into the living room and sat on the sofa next to Oliver.

Oliver said, "Before you start stuffing those biscuits into your mouth, tell me what happened when you went back to Brimstone. I want to know everything."

I told Oliver every detail starting with my visit to Blythe's house and how she was having a meeting with the fairies.

Oliver listened quietly and then said, "Yes, there is something different in the air in Brimstone. I noticed that the last time I went there with Esther. Whatever the problem is, Blythe will sort it out. What happened when you went to see the werewolves?"

I filled Oliver in about my conversation with Strom, my run-in with Flint, the chat with Tansy, and my talk with Luca. I didn't tell him I'd been mad at Luca after he kindly offered to help me. I was still embarrassed about that.

I finished my conversation by telling Oliver about the missing butterflies and the feelings I got from the tree.

Oliver looked at me for a few moments as if he were studying me. He said, "You've done an excellent job today. You went with your gut instincts, especially when it came to touching the butterfly tree. That is very weird about them going missing. I can't remember a time when they all went missing before, except for that fateful day when you and Luca caused chaos with your prank."

"I don't want to talk about that." I dunked my biscuit in my tea.

A little chuckling noise came from Oliver. "It was funny. Anyway, getting back to the werewolves. I've spoken to Strom a few times, and I'm surprised he would willingly give up his position as the alpha male. There are rumours he's killed other werewolves in the past who've tried to take that position from him. For Strom to give that up easily to someone like Jonathan Tidewell doesn't make any sense. Jonathan was still considered an outsider. And as for that nasty Flint, don't get me started on him! I've heard many horror stories about what he gets up to when he changes into a wolf. I won't give you the details as I'm worried I will frighten you away from Brimstone forever."

"Do you think it's possible that Strom killed Jonathan?" I picked my other biscuit up, dunked it in my tea, and quickly put half of the sodden, delicious mess in my mouth.

Oliver nodded his little furry head. "It's entirely possible. Getting evidence, on the other paw, is going to be a difficult task. I think you should talk to Anju and see how she feels about this matter. She might be able to give you full details of Jonathan's whereabouts before his murder took place. Also, considering what Anju does tell you, you could ask her about Jonathan's state of mind before he died. Perhaps he confided in Anju about what was worrying him."

I nodded. "For all we know, Jonathan could have received threats from either Strom or Flint. Either one could have been unhappy about the forthcoming marriage."

"Good point," Oliver said. "I've met Anju a few times, and she's one of the nicer werewolves. At least, she never looks at me as if I'm a delicious snack."

I put the rest of the biscuit in my mouth and washed it down with a big slurp of tea.

I said to Oliver, "We don't know much about the murder itself. I know Jonathan was found hanging from a tree, but if he had been forced onto the tree wouldn't there be defensive marks somewhere on his body as he tried to protect himself? Wouldn't a post-mortem show this? That's what happens on the TV crime shows. Someone will think a person has committed suicide, but then as soon as the doctor gets to work, they'll soon see it was murder."

Oliver shook his head. "If only it were that easy. Werewolves bury their dead immediately, and I suspect that's what happened with Jonathan. In fact, I'm sure that's what your Gran told me about him."

"Why would they do that?"

Oliver's nose twitched. "Not to put too fine a point on it, werewolves start to smell the moment they die. It's not a pleasant odour and it can be smelled miles away."

"Couldn't Jonathan's body be dug up again so that a post-mortem can take place?"

"Good luck with asking the werewolves about that," Oliver said. "No, once a werewolf is buried, that's it. I think your best bet is to talk to Anju and take it from there. I can come to Brimstone with you and help if you like?"

I thought about Luca's offer of help, and how quick I'd been to dismiss it. I smiled at Oliver and said, "I would love to have your help, thank you."

There was a rattle at the front door, and I recognised the sound. It was the cat flap opening.

Oliver jumped off the sofa and said, "Have we got a visitor? I'm not expecting anyone. Are you?"

"Not someone who fits through the cat flap."

We waited, and a second later we heard the heavy padding of weary paws across the carpet. I knew that sound.

Stanley came into the room, walked over to the sofa and sat down with a heavy sigh.

Oliver stared at him and suddenly yelled, "Stanley! What has happened to you? You look awful. You're so skinny, and what's happened to your lovely fur? It's gone all grey." Oliver turned an accusing stare my way and went on, "What have you done to Stanley? You've broken him."

I said, "Broken him? What do you mean? I take good care of Stanley, don't I?" I looked at Stanley as if he would understand my question.

Oliver walked closer to Stanley and looked him up and down. "Stanley, brother, tell me everything."

Stanley looked in my direction, and then back at Oliver.

Oliver said to him, "It's alright, she can hear me talking now. It's safe for you to talk to her too."

Stanley was going to talk to me? My Stanley? I took another big drink of tea and then put my cup down. I wanted to give Stanley my full attention if he was going to talk to me.

Stanley cleared his throat, looked at me and said shyly, "Hello, Cassia."

I don't know what came over me next. I don't know whether it was a combination of my lovely Stanley talking to me, or the way his voice was so soft and so sad. Whatever it was, I burst into tears.

As I tried to compose myself, I heard Oliver say to Stanley, "Give her a minute or two. She's having a very emotional day."

I finally got myself together, gave Stanley a watery smile and said, "Hello, Stanley. It's lovely to hear you speaking. How did you get here? Our apartment is miles away. What are you doing here?"

Stanley heaved himself to his feet and climbed slowly on to the sofa. He settled down next to me and said, "I had a feeling I was needed here. I walked here following the scent of you and your car. I hope I'm not troubling you." He moved a bit closer, sniffed my sleeve and added, "You've been to Brimstone again. I can smell it on you. I could smell it yesterday too."

I could only nod. I was finding it hard to speak. My lovely, beautiful, skinny cat was talking to me. His voice was so soft and apologetic.

Oliver began to pace up and down in front of the sofa. He said to Stanley, "Yes, she's been to Brimstone. Let me get you up to date with everything."

Oliver quickly filled Stanley in on what had been happening. Stanley moved even closer to me and put his little paw on my knee as if comforting me.

When Oliver had finished, he said, "So, you see Stanley, Cassia will have to go back to Brimstone. I'll go with her and help her."

Stanley said, "I can help her. I am her familiar after all." He looked up at me and added, "If you want me to? I'll try not to get in the way."

Oliver cried out, "No! You're not going anywhere with Cassia. Look at what she's done to you since you've been living together. She's almost killed you."

"I haven't!" I defended myself. "I take good care of Stanley. I look after him, and I talk to him every day."

Stanley nodded, and said, "Cassia tells me about her day every evening when she comes home from work. She has many troubles, and she shares them all with me. She also tells me about her health problems. She's going through a very stressful time."

"Stressful time?" Oliver said. "That's her fault. If she'd remembered she was a witch years ago, then she wouldn't be going through stressful times. And as for telling you all her troubles every evening, no wonder you're looking so unhappy, Stanley. She's passed all her troubles on to you."

I felt a lump of guilt in my throat. I looked down at Stanley and said, "Is that true? Have I made you depressed? Is that why you go to so many funerals? Are you feeling suicidal?"

Oliver stopped pacing and shouted, "Funerals! Yes, we've heard about the funerals. Stanley, explain yourself."

Stanley lowered his head. "It's all my fault that Cassia hadn't remembered she's a witch. If I was a proper witch's familiar, I would have made her realise it years ago. But I'm a failure. I've been having suicidal thoughts. I thought if I ended my life, Cassia could get a better cat, one who's up to the job."

"Oh, Stanley." My voice caught in my throat.

He continued, " I thought that by hanging around funerals, I might catch whatever had killed that person." He turned his little face towards me and mumbled, "I'm sorry Cassia, I've let you down."

I pulled Stanley onto my knee, and fresh tears trickled down my cheeks. "Oh, Stanley, it's not your fault at all. It's my fault."

Stanley said, "No, it's my fault."

Oliver said in exasperated tones, "You're both at fault! You idiots!"

I stroked the top of Stanley's head and said to him, "Oliver's right, we have been idiots. But we can put all that behind us now. I've remembered I'm a witch, and I'd love for you to keep being my familiar. We'll go back to Brimstone together and deal with this murder investigation. What do you say?"

Stanley lifted his chin and said, "I think that's a marvellous idea. Are we going to stay here in Esther's house now? I hope you don't mind me saying so, but I don't like our apartment."

"I don't like it either. Yes, we'll stay here for a little while. I'll tell you what, Stanley, I'll go back to the apartment now and collect some of our things."

"That's an excellent idea," Stanley said.

I tickled him behind his ears and said, "It certainly is."

I had a spring in my step as I returned to my apartment a short while later. But all the joy ran out of me as I stepped into my apartment and found someone sitting on my sofa. It wasn't a talking cat this time.

Chapter 17

Alistair was sitting on my sofa drinking from a bottle of water. His jacket was flung over the back of the sofa, and his feet were propped up on the table in front of him. He was watching something on the television. He'd made himself very much at home. Anger flared in my stomach. Alastair was really annoying me today.

He didn't look over in my direction as he said, "At last. I've been waiting ages for you. Where've you been?"

"I see you've let yourself in."

Still with his eyes on the television screen, he said, "Of course I've let myself in. What's the point of having a spare key if I don't use it?" He pointed the remote control at the TV and paused the programme he was watching. He turned his head in my direction and continued, "Well? Where have you been and what have you been doing? I've been leaving messages on your phone all day. I could see from the app on my phone that you've been at your gran's house all day. What's so important there? Why haven't you returned any of my calls or replied to my messages? This won't do, Cassia, this won't do at all."

I walked further into the apartment and tried to get rid of the anger which was simmering away in my stomach like a small fire. Calmly, I said, "I've been at Gran's house looking after her. I left work abruptly because it was an emergency."

Alistair snorted. "Emergency or not, you should have kept me up to date on what you were doing. You should have returned my messages. Don't I mean anything to you? And it was so unprofessional of you to leave the office so abruptly without telling me. I had to find out from Cheryl. It's not good enough."

I didn't reply as I walked over to the fridge and opened the door. I reached for a bottle of water and immediately noticed my last yoghurt had been taken. I knew it wasn't Stanley, so that could only leave one culprit.

Alistair carried on, "What exactly is wrong with your gran this time? Did she need help with a knitting pattern or something?" This was followed by a snort of derision.

I unscrewed the top of the water bottle and turned around to face Alistair. "She'd had a fall and was hurt. She needed me to look after her. In fact, I'm going to take time off work so I can look after her properly."

"Seriously? Why? You can hire someone to do that sort of thing. You have to get back to work. You've already taken time off for personal reasons, and you know that is frowned upon. Remember Cassia, your work reflects on me. Speaking of which, you didn't show me the appraisals before they were handed in. I only found out later that Cheryl had brought them up to the top floor on your behalf."

"I didn't have time to tell you about them. Like I said, Gran was hurt and I wanted to get to her quickly. I don't see what the problem is. The appraisals were finished and delivered on time."

Alistair retorted, "But I needed to see them before they went to the top floor to make sure you hadn't made any stupid mistakes. I did get to look at them later, even though it was too late to make any changes. You'd done an okay job, but you used some expressions that I wouldn't have used. Next time, make sure I get see them first. We can discuss it fully tomorrow when you come back to work."

The rage inside me increased, and I was afraid I was going to erupt like some human volcano. My hand tightened around the bottle of water, and I said, "Alistair,

I won't be coming into work tomorrow. I'm going to look after Gran, and that's that." I was almost tempted to add that I would be dealing with the murder of a werewolf too.

"You can't take time off work for personal reasons, Cassia. How would that look?"

I shrugged. "I'll use some of my holidays. I've got plenty of holiday time left."

Anger flickered in Alistair's eyes. "We always take our holidays together. I've already got plans for our next holiday. If you use some of your days up now, that will spoil my plans. Look, we'll discuss this over dinner. I've booked a table at my favourite restaurant, and we need to be there in an hour's time. That's enough time for you to clean yourself up and to do something with your make-up and hair." He turned his back on me and pointed the remote control at the TV. "That gives me time to finish watching this documentary I've recorded. Stop differing, Cassia, I don't want to lose our reservation."

I put the bottle of water down as I was afraid I was going to fling it at Alistair. A sudden, painful throbbing came into my head, and that was accompanied by the familiar acidic twinges in my stomach. My ulcers had decided to say hello. They'd been quiet all day. What had triggered them?

I looked towards the sofa. Had Alistair always spoken to me in such a dismissive manner? If so, I only had myself to blame by allowing him to do so. Well, that couldn't go on any longer. Things had to change. An image of Gran's face came into my mind, and I thought about her secret life. She'd been dealing with it all on her own. The image of Stanley's little furry face followed Gran's. What had I done to that poor cat?

I stood up straight, and a sensation of calmness descended on me. I knew without doubt what I had to do next.

I walked over to the sofa, grabbed Alistair's jacket and tapped him on the shoulder. I said to him, "Alistair, I am taking time off work, and there's no point arguing about it. I am not going to dinner with you as I have other plans."

"What plans? You never have any plans."

My plans involved dealing with the suspicious death of a werewolf in a magical land called Brimstone, but I wasn't going to tell Alistair that. Instead, I said, "I've got plans to look after Gran. Here's your jacket." I waved it in the air in case he hadn't seen it.

Alistair reluctantly got to his feet and took the jacket. "I'm disappointed in you, Cassia. This is most unlike you. You're not thinking about my feelings whatsoever. After all I've done for you and your career. You know I only want the best for you. That's why I wanted to talk to you tonight about our future. I've given a lot of thought to it, and I've even made bullet points on my phone of the things I want to talk about."

He quickly looked away but not before I saw the hurt in his eyes. My resolve immediately softened, and I felt sympathy for him. It was true that he only had my best interests at heart.

Alistair shrugged into his jacket and looked back at me. His tone was softer as he said, "I know I can be an idiot at times, but I do care a great deal for you. I'm sorry if I'm being too forceful. Of course, you need to look after your gran. Let me know how you get on. We can talk about our future another time." He leant over and pecked me on the cheek. "I'll see myself out. Take care." He quickly left the apartment.

I turned towards the television, picked up the remote and pressed stop. I felt so guilty now about Alistair, but I knew it was for the best. I'd deal with our relationship problems later. I had too many other things to deal with now.

I spent the next thirty minutes packing my belongings into a suitcase along with the small things that Stanley would need. I took all the perishable food from the fridge and packed those too. I wasn't sure how long I was going to be away, but it was going to be more than a day or two. As I was packing my bag, a feeling of lightness flowed through me along with a sense of excitement. It felt like I was going on a great adventure.

I left a message with the appropriate people at work, followed by email confirmation. I hoped my sudden absence wouldn't cause too many problems. I knew Cheryl was more than capable of dealing with my workload. I made a mental note to buy her a huge thank you present.

I had no qualms about leaving the apartment, and as I closed the door behind me, I realised it had never felt like home anyway. Gran's house was my home. Gran hadn't changed a thing in my room at her house and had left everything untouched in case I wanted to come back. Had she been hoping I would someday embrace my witch side? When I had time, I would have a long conversation with her about it.

My heart still felt light as I drove back to Gran's house and let myself in. Oliver was waiting for me.

He said, "Esther is awake, and she wants to talk to you urgently."

Chapter 18

Gran was sitting up in bed and looking much happier when I walked into her bedroom. The makeshift book weights had gone from her cover, and she didn't show any signs of floating off the bed.

Gran's face lit up when she saw me. "Cassia! It's so good to see you back. We've got a lot to talk about, haven't we?" She patted the side of her bed. "Sit yourself down. Before we start chatting, have you still got that levitating potion with you? Blythe knows me so well. She knows I can't bear to keep still and that levitating potion will help me as I go about my chores."

"You shouldn't be doing any chores at all. Dr Gilbert told you to rest."

"Pah! What does he know? Have you got the potion?"

I reached into my pocket and retrieved the small bottle. I placed it on the bedside table and then settled myself down next to Gran on the bed. It was a huge bed, and there was plenty of room for both of us.

Gran said, "Before we begin, Oliver's told me everything that you told him when I was asleep. Despite me telling you not to get yourself involved, you went ahead and did it anyway."

I couldn't meet her gaze, and I looked at the bedcover instead. "Are you mad?"

Gran gave me a friendly shoulder bump and said, "Of course not. I'm glad you did it. I've been trying to protect you for so long, and it was the wrong thing to do. You look more alive now than you have done for months. Do you want to continue dealing with the case? If so, there are many questions to be asked when you go back to Brimstone."

I looked up from the bedcover and gave Gran a smile. "I'd love to continue dealing with it. Did Oliver tell you about Flint? He's my number one suspect at the moment."

Gran nodded. "Yes, I'm not surprised Flint is your number one suspect. I'm concerned about the butterflies disappearing. I hope they return soon as Brimstone won't be the same without them."

"Do you think they've gone into a different world? I didn't have the chance to tell you earlier, but a Brimstone butterfly came into my office this morning with a message from you. I heard you crying for help."

Gran frowned. "Really? I don't remember sending a message, but I must have. And I'm not sure how a butterfly made its way into your office. They are clever creatures, though."

"Gran, if it's not too upsetting to talk about it, can you remember anything about your attack?"

"Yes, I can remember some things. I was on my way through the forest to talk to Strom. It was Strom who'd voiced concerns to Blythe about Jonathan's death. He had his reservations about it not being suicide. Apparently, it was Flint who found Jonathan's body hanging from the tree, and with his werewolf friends, he buried Jonathan in the pack cemetery immediately. His excuse was that he wanted to spare Anju any upset."

My eyes narrowed. "That sounds like a feeble excuse. Sounds like he was trying to hide any incriminating evidence."

"Indeed. Blythe's suspicions were immediately raised when Strom told her this, and she asked Strom if any of the other werewolves had actually seen Jonathan hanging from the tree. Strom said they had, and he believes them. So, it wasn't just Flint who saw Jonathan."

I shook my head. "It still sounds suspicious."

"I agree. That was one of the questions I was going to raise with Strom. On the way through the forest, I headed towards the oak tree where Jonathan had died."

"Were you on your own? Oliver told me he helps you with your work."

"I didn't have Oliver with me as he doesn't like the werewolves and how they look at him. He tries to be brave whenever we meet them, but I know how uneasy they make him feel. I wish now that I'd brought him with me as he might have alerted me to danger. He's good at that. Anyway, I was on my way to the oak tree when I heard some voices. I was going to ignore the voices until one of them mentioned Jonathan's name. I moved closer, and I saw Flint and Anju standing by the oak tree. Anju was resting her head against Flint's chest, and she was crying quietly. Flint was stroking her hair, and he was saying it was for the best that Jonathan had gone. He went on to say that Jonathan wasn't anything like them and never would have been. He added it was a blessing in disguise and Anju would see that some day. Anju didn't say anything; she just continued to cry."

"How dare he say that to her? That's so insensitive."

Gran nodded. "Exactly. That was my thought too. Flint started to say something else, but I couldn't hear him properly, so I moved a bit closer. But then I stepped on a twig, and it broke. I don't know what it is about that area in the forest, but there are millions of dried out twigs scattered across the ground. You can't help but step on them and break them. It's almost like someone has put them there on purpose as a warning system.

"Anyway, as soon as I made that noise with the twig, Flint raised his head and looked in my direction. I could see his nostrils flaring and knew he was trying to pick up my scent. I didn't want to be caught spying, so I turned away and started to quickly head back down the path. I'd only been walking for about ten seconds or so when I felt someone push me from behind. I went tumbling down a verge, and even though I put my hands out to stop myself, I couldn't. I remember landing against something hard, and the next thing I knew I was back home and lying on my sofa. Dr Gilbert was looking down at me and, well, you know the rest. I don't know who attacked me, but I'm going to find out who it was."

I said, "I'm going to find out too. And I want to find out who brought you back home and then phoned Dr Gilbert."

Gran patted my hand. "That's my girl. I like the determination in your voice. I know you're ready to deal with this case on my behalf. Even though you haven't had your full witch training yet, I know you'll be alright." Uncertainty crossed her face. "Yes, I'm sure you'll be alright. We're Winter witches, and we have respect in Brimstone. Yes, you'll be alright. I'm sure of it."

I couldn't help but say, "Someone didn't show any respect to you when they shoved you down that verge."

Gran's eyes narrowed. "Indeed. When I find out who it was, they'll be getting a piece of my mind and the sharp side of my tongue. Anyway, let's not think about that for now. I agree with Oliver that you should speak to Anju next. It's too late to go back to Brimstone now; you can do that tomorrow. Do you agree?"

"Yes, I do."

Gran squeezed my hand. "Good. Right, let's forget all about werewolves and suspicious deaths. Let's watch something on the TV. Can you bring up the box set of Miss Marple, please? We can watch it up here on the portable TV. And how about phoning for a Chinese takeaway? Get me some extra fried rice. I'm starving."

I smiled at Gran, glad to see her back to her former self. I left the room and was soon organising everything for our evening.

We had a lovely evening together sitting on Gran's bed and watching Miss Marple solve the mystery of the murder in the vicarage. We put the food on trays and managed to eat up every morsel of it. I'd been keeping a close eye on everything I ate for the last year, so it was a relief to just tuck in and enjoy my food without thinking about calories and fat content. Oliver and Stanley settled themselves at the foot of Gran's bed and watched TV with us.

Gran fell asleep before the mystery was solved. I removed the trays and tucked the bedcover around her. I had a quick tidy up and then went to my room. I snuggled down in my wonderfully comfy bed. I was asleep within minutes and had the best night's sleep I'd had in months.

I woke up the next morning ready for anything.

Chapter 19

The plan today was to locate Anju and to talk to her about Jonathan. I wanted to find out more about her relationship with him, and how he'd been feeling and acting shortly before his death. It wasn't going to be an easy conversation.

I made Gran her favourite breakfast of scrambled eggs on toast and, along with a cup of tea, I took it upstairs to her. She was sitting up in bed and watching breakfast television when I entered her room.

She pointed to the screen and said, "Have you seen what's going on today? Those politicians are lying to us again. I wish I could give them a truth potion, and then we'd see their true colours! I can't watch it any longer." She pointed the remote control at the television and switched it off. She looked me over and said, "You look refreshed this morning. I think the bags under your eyes have almost gone."

I wasn't sure if that was a compliment or not. "I've brought you some breakfast if you feel like eating."

Gran grinned at me and patted her stomach. "I'm starving. This recovery business makes you hungry. Thank you, Cassia."

I put the tray on Gran's lap, and she was soon tucking in. I sat in the chair at the side of the bed and asked how she was feeling, although it was obvious she was much better.

With her cheeks bulging with food she said, "I feel fantastic. A bit sore in places, and my ankle feels tender, but other than that, I'm raring to go."

I shot her a wary look. "Raring to go? You're not going anywhere. The doctor said you have to take it easy. Where exactly are you planning on going?"

Gran averted her gaze and gave her full attention to her breakfast. "Nowhere. But, if you were planning on going to Brimstone, I thought I might come with you and give you some pointers with your investigation."

I put my hand on Gran's arm, and she looked my way. I said to her, "I'm not going to learn how to do my investigations with you at my side. It would be better if I did this on my own. You can see that, can't you?"

Gran shrugged. "I suppose so. Don't put yourself in any danger, though."

I smiled at her. "I wasn't intending to. Anyway, I'll have Stanley with me."

Gran shook her head. "I can't believe how skinny and grey that cat has become. You should have told me how bad he was."

"I didn't realise. He looks even worse when he stands next to Oliver. Gran, is Stanley beyond repair?" My guilt about Stanley was still there like an uncomfortable, heavy stone in my stomach.

Gran waved her fork at me. "He'll be right as rain soon. Like you, he's back where he belongs."

I sat with Gran, and we chatted until she'd finished her breakfast. I asked her what her plans were for the day, and again, she averted her gaze from me and said she'd float around the house doing small jobs.

She caught my worried look and added, "There's no need to be so concerned. I can take care of myself. I'll use Blythe's levitation potion sparingly. You can't expect me to sit in bed all day shouting at the television." She flapped her hand at me and continued, "Off you go then. Let me know how you get on. And, be careful out there."

I stood up and picked the tray up. "You've already told me to be careful twice. I will be. See you later."

I went back to the kitchen and washed up before getting myself ready to enter Brimstone. I packed my bag with a bottle of water and a notepad. I stuck a couple of chocolate bars in there too in case I needed a boost of energy. I also put in some packets of cat snacks for Stanley which he loved.

Stanley padded into the kitchen, lifted his chin and said, "Good morning, Cassia. Sorry for having a lie in, but I had a wonderful night's sleep. Oliver and I stayed up for a while too, we were chatting and catching up with things. It's good to be home, isn't it?"

"It is, Stanley. Are you ready to go to Brimstone now?"

"I am. I've already had some breakfast with Oliver. We had sardines. They were delicious."

I smiled down at him and was relieved to hear that he was eating again. He'd barely touched his food these last few months.

We went down to the cellar and over to the door. Oliver was sitting there with what looked like an impatient expression on his face. For a cat, he had a great variety of expressions.

Oliver said, "Right, are we ready?"

I said, "Yes, Stanley and I are ready. You weren't thinking of coming with us, were you?"

Oliver gave me a sharp nod and said, "Of course I'm coming with you. You and Stanley have no idea what you're doing. You're going to make mistakes."

I replied, "Yes, we are going to make mistakes. That's how we'll learn. Oliver, thanks for your offer of help, but we have to do this on our own. You do understand, don't you?"

Oliver studied me for a few seconds, and then gave a disdainful sniff. He mumbled, "I suppose so. Open the door and at least let me have a look outside to make sure the coast is clear."

I moved the table I'd placed in front of the door to one side and then opened the door. The lovely fresh smell from Brimstone wafted in. It was that same mixture of exciting smells like a summer's morning and a winter's evening all mixed together. The smell of adventure.

Oliver stuck his head through the open door, and his whiskers twitched. He looked back at me and said, "You'll find Anju in Mooncrest Café. It's down there on the left."

I gave him an impressed look. "How do you know that? Do you have magical abilities?"

"No, I just saw her walking into the café. She appears to be on her own." He took a couple of steps back and said, "I suppose you two had better go then, if you don't need my help."

I ignored his hurt tone and turned to Stanley. I raised my eyebrows in question. He gave me a nod of confirmation, and we stepped through the cellar door and on to the cobbled pathway.

I closed the door behind me, but not before hearing Oliver shout out, "Be careful out there!"

Stanley and I stood for a minute in silence while we took in the scene before us.

I looked down at Stanley and said, "Well? What do you think about Brimstone?"

Stanley replied, "It's wonderful. Just as wonderful as I remember it."

"You've been here before? When?"

Stanley replied, "I used to come here with you when you were a little girl, don't you remember? We used to run around the square together. We had some marvellous adventures." There was a hurt tone in his voice now.

I leant down and stroked Stanley's head. "I'm sorry, Stanley, there's a lot that I can't remember. I don't mean to hurt your feelings. Have you been back here recently?"

"No, I stopped coming here when you did. I have missed it, though."

I straightened up, and we walked along the cobbled path. We stopped at the butterfly tree. It was still devoid of butterflies. I glanced at the other butterfly trees around the square, and noticed with a sinking heart they were still empty too. Where had those butterflies gone?

We walked towards the town square and passed the road that led to Blythe's house. I wondered if she was in. I could do with having a talk with her. Perhaps we'd get the chance to visit her later.

As we walked along, Stanley said, "Cassia, do you think it's safe for us to be here? I feel as if people are giving us funny looks. Do you think they mean to cause us harm?"

I took a quick scan of the town square, and even though there were many residents walking around, I couldn't see that anyone in particular was giving us their attention. Or were they? Was Stanley picking up on something?

We went into Mooncrest Café, and I was struck immediately by how bright and cheerful it was. The walls were painted in a light yellow, and there were images of trees and flowers on them. It almost felt as if we were still outside. Then I noticed the customers sitting at the wooden tables. There was a myriad of creatures in many different shades of skin colour including green and purple. There were pointy ears, elongated noses, bushy whiskers, furry faces and lots of fangs. I took a sharp intake of breath. Many, many sets of fangs were bared in our direction as customers looked our way. Were they giving us welcoming smiles or a warning snarl?

Stanley nudged my leg and said quietly, "They're staring at us. They want to eat us. This is a dangerous place. Let's go."

I whispered back, "We can't go. We have to talk to Anju. I don't even know what she looks like. Do you?"

Stanley lifted his chin and said, "I'll try and sniff her out."

I waited a moment while Stanley's whiskers twitched. After a little while, he padded towards a wooden table at the far side of the café. He jumped onto a chair at the side of a young woman. That must be Anju then.

Ignoring the hostile, or friendly, stares that came from the creatures in the room, I walked towards the table.

I stopped at the side of it, and said politely, "Hello, sorry for disturbing you. I'm Cassia Winter. Would you mind if I spoke to you for a while?"

I quickly took in Anju's appearance. The most striking part of her was her long, wavy hair. It was an amazing burnished copper colour, and it shone as if it had been polished. It reminded me of some of the pans in Gran's kitchen which she lovingly cleaned once a month. I was almost tempted to lean forward to see if I could make out my reflection in Anju's hair. Even though she was sitting down, I could see she had that scarily athletic build going on and her muscles strained against the sleeves of her T-shirt.

Anju turned brown eyes my way, and I saw they were red-rimmed as if she'd been crying a lot recently.

Anju said, "I know who you are, and I know why you want to talk to me. I'm going to save you a lot of trouble and tell you Jonathan's death was entirely my fault."

Chapter 20

I took a seat opposite Anju, moved my head closer to hers, and said quietly, "Did you kill Jonathan?"

"As good as. It was my fault that Jonathan was in our world. If he hadn't been in our world, then he'd still be alive and well in his own world."

I was about to ask her another question when a tall, thin creature appeared at my side. She was so pale that she was almost translucent.

The creature spoke, "Good morning, I'm Gilda. I'm your waitress today. Let me get your order."

I looked around the table for a menu but couldn't find one. I said to Gilda, "I haven't decided what I want yet. Is there a menu somewhere?"

Gilda let out a tinkle of a laugh and explained, "We don't need menus here. Everything you want is in your head. As this is your first time here, let me show you how it works. Don't panic."

Why is it when anyone says, 'Don't panic', you immediately do?

I stiffened as Gilda moved a long, thin hand towards me. She rested it on my shoulder, closed her eyes for a second, and then opened her eyes. She said, "A cup of tea and a toasted teacake with butter. Am I right?"

I stared in astonishment at her. That's exactly what I'd been thinking. Even though I'd made sure Gran had eaten this morning, I'd forgotten to feed myself.

I said to Gilda, "Are you a mind reader?" I immediately tried to clear my mind of thoughts about how thin and tall she was. If she could read my mind, I didn't want her to be insulted by my thoughts.

Gilda laughed again. "Sort of. I'm very good at picking up on what our customers would like to eat and drink." She turned her attention to Stanley, her long arm reached out, and she gently placed it on his back. She gave him a smile and said, "Of course. I'll get that for you." She then floated away from us as if she were on wheels.

I wanted to ask Anju who and what Gilda was, but now didn't seem the appropriate time.

"Anju, can you tell me more about Jonathan and why you feel so guilty about him, please?"

She gave me a small nod and began, "Jonathan was bitten by a werewolf called Gregor. Gregor was a friend of mine, and I knew he had a wild side. Gregor wasn't very good at controlling his werewolf self, and he had to be locked in a cage when there was a full moon. He hated being stuck in a cage, and he always pleaded with me to let him out. I knew that wasn't a possibility as Gregor couldn't control his killing urges once he was free. Everyone in the pack knew that.

"But over time, Gregor seemed to change, and he appeared to be in control of himself more. We'd often spend time together, and he convinced me that he had made positive changes. When it came time for him to be locked up during a full moon, he pleaded with me to unlock the cage so that he could test out his newly acquired control skills. After our many chats together, I thought he really had changed." She looked down at her hands which were resting on the table. "Big mistake."

"What happened?"

Anju turned tear-filled eyes my way, and continued, "Gregor might have thought he'd changed his ways when he was in human form, but as soon as he turned into his wolf form, he was different. He was wild and out of control; more than ever before. I opened the cage door that night just as he was turning, and when he'd fully transformed, I expected him to be as controlled as everyone else. But he wasn't. Once he'd changed, he howled in such an angry way that it made my hackles rise with fear. I've never heard any wolf make that noise before. He pushed me to one side and then ran off into the forest still making that terrible noise. I realised my mistake immediately and went to tell my father. You met him yesterday, didn't you? Strom?"

I nodded.

Anju said, "My father was furious with me, and he went after Gregor. It was too late. My father tracked Gregor's scent and discovered he'd gone through the darkest part of the forest and into the human world. That is completely forbidden. My father had no option but to follow Gregor. And when he did, he discovered that Gregor had slain a family; Jonathan's family. Jonathan's wife and young son had been killed outright, but Jonathan was still alive, albeit with wolf bites. My father took pity on Jonathan and brought him back to our pack."

I asked, "Is it true that Gregor was killed afterwards? That's what your father told me yesterday."

Anju nodded. "My father had no option. He had to do it. When my father brought Jonathan back, along with Gregor's dead body, he took the blame for Gregor's escape. He said he hadn't secured his cage properly. He didn't want anyone to know it was my fault." She lowered her head. "I felt so ashamed. I was the reason why Jonathan's family had been killed."

"What happened to Jonathan when he was brought into your pack?"

"I was the one who took care of him. I had to. It was my fault he was there. He was in a bad way for a few days. Because he'd been bitten by a werewolf, his healing abilities sped up, and he was soon back to physical health. But his mental health was another matter.

"On the first day that I looked after him, I confessed what I'd done. There was a coldness in Jonathan's eyes when I did so, and I didn't blame him for hating me. Jonathan was of a strong character, and he had a decency about him which I'd never encountered before. We began to talk more, and he said it wasn't my fault that Gregor had attacked his family. He said Gregor was probably the kind of werewolf who would have escaped from a cage eventually. I told him repeatedly it was my fault, but after a time, Jonathan wouldn't listen to my declarations of guilt. He even forgave me for the part I'd played in Gregor escaping. He was that kind of man."

Gilda floated back to our table and placed a steaming mug of tea and a hot buttered teacake in front of me. I felt my mouth watering, and I quickly wiped away a dribble of saliva that escaped from the corner of my mouth. Gilda put a small plate of sardines in front of Stanley. His little pink tongue shot out, and he licked his lips. I wasn't the only one who was dribbling.

Gilda said, "Don't worry about settling the bill, your gran has an account with us." She smiled before moving away.

I smiled at Stanley and said, "More sardines? Haven't you had enough of them?"

Stanley said, "I can't help it, I love them. If I keep eating them at this rate, I'll turn into a sardine myself." He let out a wheezy sort of chuckle which was incredibly charming. My heart swelled with love for my furry feline friend.

I said to Anju, "Stanley said he might turn into a sardine."

"I know, I heard him."

"Oh? I thought hearing cats talk was a witch thing." I felt a stab of disappointment.

Anju looked Stanley's way, gave him a small smile, and said, "Everyone can hear cats talking here. Stanley, what a lovely cat you are. I can sense how much you care about Cassia."

Stanley let out a purr in response.

I took a drink of tea before asking Anju my next question. "How did the rest of your pack deal with Jonathan coming in?"

"They dealt with it well, for the most part. There was an immense feeling of guilt about what Gregor had done, and we all wanted to make amends. Apart from one person who didn't like the attention I was giving Jonathan."

"Don't tell me, was it Flint?"

Anju nodded. "Yes, it was Flint. From your tone, I'm assuming you've met him. Once someone meets Flint, they never forget him. Flint showed nothing but hatred towards Jonathan. Jonathan took it in his stride and did his best to make friends with Flint. But Flint wasn't having any of it."

"I'd heard that you and Flint were in a relationship at some point." I picked up the warm teacake and took a big bite while waiting for Anju to answer. The bread was soft, and the butter was deliciously salty. My taste buds did a little happy dance. I made a mental note to ask Gilda if I could buy some teacakes to take home. Gran would love these. Perhaps she was a regular visitor here and already had a stash of teacakes at home? I'd ask her later.

Anju said, "Yes, I was in a relationship with Flint. It wasn't a healthy relationship. Even though Flint was rough and controlling with me, I thought that's how things were supposed to be. Until I met Jonathan, and got to know him better. His caring attitude and thoughtful ways were a stark contrast to how Flint behaved, and slowly, I fell in love with Jonathan.

"As soon as I realised I had feelings for Jonathan, I ended things with Flint. He didn't take it well, and his hatred for Jonathan intensified. I've no idea how it happened, considering the whole Gregor incident, but Jonathan began to fall in love with me. How he got over the death of his family is still a mystery to me. He told me that terrible things happen in life, and we either deal with them or let them rule us. Jonathan said he would never forget his family and would always carry them in his heart. But, he had to accept his new life and make the best of it."

I swallowed the last of the teacake before asking, "How did your father feel about Jonathan?"

"My father admired Jonathan. Jonathan proved his worth around our community by doing more than his fair share of work. He also went out into the wider community and offered his services there. The others who live in the forest always distrusted our pack and kept their distance. Jonathan began to change that with his gentle ways. He was doing us a great favour. He's going to be sorely missed by many of us in Brimstone." A solitary tear trickled down her cheek.

Despite Anju's distress, I had to continue with my questions. "I spoke to Tansy yesterday, and she told me Jonathan wasn't acting himself recently. Is that true?"

"It is. He started to act differently shortly after our engagement. I knew he wasn't sleeping well as I often heard him moving about the camp in the early hours of the morning. At first, he didn't want to talk about what was bothering him, but I insisted that he told me. He explained he couldn't stop thinking about his wife and son, and he was having constant nightmares about them. He felt their deaths were entirely his fault. I tried to reassure him, but it was hard. He said it was probably just a temporary thing, and he'd do his best to deal with it. But he didn't deal with it. Things seem to get worse for him, and he was barely sleeping at all. Whenever I tried to talk about his nightmares, he'd change the subject and talk about our future instead." More tears travelled down her cheeks.

Stanley jumped onto Anju's lap and he pressed his head against her shoulder. He purred softly, and Anju stroked his back.

As loath as I was to bring up the subject of Gran's attack, I knew I had to.

"Anju, I'm sorry to mention this, but my Gran saw you and Flint together near the oak tree where Jonathan died. Gran was attacked shortly after that. Do you know anything about the attack?"

Anju blinked away a tear and opened her mouth. She never got the chance to speak as someone laid a heavy hand on my shoulder and snarled, "Leave her alone! You've done enough damage already. Look at her. She's distressed. Get yourself out of here immediately, Cassia Winter, before I throw you out."

I looked up into the dark eyes of Flint.

Anju said, "Flint, don't talk to Cassia like that. She's trying to find out the truth about Jonathan."

Without taking his eyes off me, Flint said, "It's werewolf business, not witch business. She's not even a proper witch. She's insulting us by thinking she can get involved in our business." He bared his teeth at me and I could have sworn I heard a low growling sound in his throat.

I shoved his hand off my shoulder and got to my feet. I was about to tell him I had every right to be investigating Jonathan's death when something out on the street caught my attention.

I turned to Stanley and said, "Stanley, we have to leave immediately."

Chapter 21

The spectacle which had caught my attention from the café, at first, appeared like a green cloud lowering over the town square. But the slight fluttering and flapping sounds coming from within the cloud told me it was the butterflies returning to Brimstone.

Stanley and I stood outside the café and watched the green cloud as it dispersed in several directions. The butterflies made their way to the various trees around the square and settled on the branches. I looked towards the butterfly tree by the cobbled path and noticed the butterflies had returned to that one too.

I said to Stanley, "Come on, let's see if the butterflies have anything to tell us."

I had no idea if I could talk to the butterflies or not, but seeing as I could now speak with cats, it was worth a try.

We walked over to the tree and stopped in front of it. I looked closer at the butterflies. Every single creature had its wings closed, and they weren't moving at all.

Stanley said, "They look sad. I can feel their sadness. Cassia, what's wrong with them?"

"I don't know." I aimed my attention at the butterflies and said gently, "Hello, can you understand me? Can you talk to me?"

There was no movement or sound from the still butterflies. I decided to try something else and placed my hands on the trunk of the tree. I closed my eyes and took in the feelings that radiated from the tree.

The world stopped around me. The breeze dropped, and it was suddenly silent. It felt like a heavy blanket of sadness was descending slowly over me. My heart ached with sadness, and I leant my head against the trunk.

I continued to take in the feelings. I can only describe it like someone turning a tap on in my heart and my happiness slowly drained away.

There was a nudge on my legs. I opened my eyes.

Stanley said to me, "Cassia! You're crying. Take your hands off the tree immediately; it's doing something horrible to you."

I took my hands off the tree and took a step back. I felt the wetness of my cheeks and I wiped my tears away. I said to Stanley, "I felt sad, really sad. It was like I'd lost something incredibly important to me. Stanley, what's going on with the butterflies? What have they lost?"

Stanley said, "Perhaps it's a case of who have they lost?"

"Who? Yes, you might be right. We need to talk to Blythe about this. She'll know what's going on here."

Stanley and I headed towards Blythe's house, and I was soon knocking on the door. Despite knocking several times, there was no answer. I walked to the nearest window and peered through. I couldn't see anyone inside, not even a small fairy.

Stanley shook his head. "What is happening in this town? There's something odd going on. I can feel it in my fur."

We walked back down the street, and I looked towards Mooncrest café. Anju stepped out, closely followed by Flint. Flint must have sensed us watching him because he looked our way and shot us a warning glance. He put his thick arm around Anju's shoulders and led her away.

Stanley said, "Cassia, what are we going to do next? Should we try and talk to Anju again?"

"Not at the moment. Something was bothering Jonathan before he died. Strom said Jonathan wouldn't take his own life, but what if he did? What if he wasn't coping with the loss of his family as he made out? Maybe he felt incredibly guilty after getting engaged to

Anju. He couldn't accept feeling happy when his family had been killed so brutally. We might not be looking at a murder case at all. It could be suicide."

Stanley interjected, "If that's the case, then who attacked your Gran and why?"

I looked in Flint and Anju's direction as they departed the square. "For all we know, it could have been Flint who attacked Gran just for the fun of it."

"That's true. What should we do now?"

I considered the matter for a moment and then said, "Let's go back home and check on Gran. I want to make sure she's okay, and it'll give me the chance to fill her in on my conversation with Anju."

We made our way back to the cellar door, checking on the butterfly tree as we went. The butterflies were still in their unmoving state.

We found Gran in the kitchen. Or more correctly, she was floating inches from the kitchen ceiling.

I put my hands on my hips and stared up at her. "Gran, what are you doing up there?"

Gran gave us a cheery smile and said, "I took a tad too much of the levitation potion."

"Do you want me to get you down? If I stand on a chair, I can grab your ankles."

Gran flapped a yellow duster at me. "Not just yet, thank you. This gives me the perfect opportunity to get to those hard to reach places." She made a swimming motion with her arms and headed over towards the corner of the room. She dabbed away at a spider's web with her duster.

I shook my head at her. "How long have you been up there? Are you in pain?"

Gran looked down at us. "I'm not in any pain at all. I feel as if I'm floating on air." She chuckled. "That's exactly what I am doing. It's great fun. Tell me about your investigation while I finish cleaning the ceiling."

I took a seat at the kitchen table and started to tell Gran about my conversation with Anju. It's very peculiar to have a conversation with an elderly woman who's floating around the ceiling cleaning up cobwebs. But I managed.

Gran made tutting noises as I told her about Flint turning up. She said, "That werewolf needs taking down a peg or two. I'll be having a word with Strom about him as soon as I'm able to. I always suspected Anju had something to do with Gregor's attack on Jonathan's family. Whenever Gregor was mentioned, she always had a guilty look on her face. Poor girl. It must be a heavy burden that she's carrying around. I met Jonathan a few times, and he was the decent sort, so I can understand how he would have forgiven Anju's part in the attack on his family."

Stanley jumped onto my lap and settled himself down. He reminded me about the butterfly incident. I told Gran that the butterflies had returned, and the feelings that had come over me as I touched the tree.

Gran descended a few inches and gave me a concerned look. "The butterflies never close their wings like that. That's most unusual. And those feelings you describe are extremely worrying. Did you speak to Blythe about it?"

I shook my head. "She wasn't in. Brin wasn't in either."

Gran descended another inch. "Not in? That is beyond peculiar. That never happens. If Blythe isn't available to see people, Brin is always there to do so. Something very weird is going on in Brimstone."

"Gran, do you want me to pull you down now?"

"Not yet. I can get to the top of the cupboards from this height. I know who you should speak to next. You should speak to Mrs Merryweather."

"Mrs Merryweather? She sounds like a nice person."

Oliver took that moment to walk in and join in with our conversation. "Mrs Merryweather? She's a gossipy goblin who can't keep her pointy nose out of other people's business."

Gran added, "Which makes her the perfect one to talk to. Everyone tells Mrs Merryweather their problems or concerns, whether they want to or not."

"What do you mean by that?" I asked. "Does she have magical abilities?"

Oliver made a snorting noise. "She wishes. No, she's just a nosy old so-and-so who lives her life through other people. Good luck talking to her. You'll need it."

Gran gave Oliver sharp look. "Just because you've had a bad experience with Mrs Merryweather doesn't mean that Cassia will."

Gran turned her attention to me. "Although, try not to spend more than five or ten minutes with Mrs Merryweather or you'll regret it."

I shifted in my chair. "What do you mean by that?"

Gran descended a few more inches and gave me a big smile. "You'll soon see. It's all good experience for you, Cassia. Go and see her right now. There's no time like the present."

I stroked Stanley's head and said to him, "Well? Do you want come with me to see a gossipy goblin?"

Stanley nodded. "Anywhere you go, I'll be right at your side."

Chapter 22

With Gran's directions, Stanley and I returned to Brimstone and made our way to the forest to find Mrs Merryweather's cottage. According to Gran, the cottage wasn't far from the oak tree where Jonathan Tidewell had died. As I'd already visited the tree before, it didn't take us long to find the cottage.

My heart lifted at the sight of the cottage. It was a charming building with a thatched roof and straw-coloured walls. There were roses blooming up and around the front door. It was the perfect cottage.

I tensed when I saw the creature standing at the front door. She wasn't at all charming. All her features were angular, from her long, pointed nose to her sharp chin. Even her ears were long, thin and pointy. She was wearing a floral dress which had a handkerchief-style hem with points aimed towards the stone path she was standing on.

With a tremor in his voice, Stanley said, "Is that Mrs Merryweather? I don't like the look of her. Are you sure we've got the right place? I can't imagine anyone telling their secrets to someone who looks that menacing."

"This is the only cottage around here, so it must be Mrs Merryweather's. I don't like the look of her either, but we have to talk to her."

Tentatively, we walked down the path and towards the goblin who was watching us with beady, calculating eyes.

My hand shook somewhat as I raised it in greeting, and I said, "Mrs Merryweather?"

The goblin nodded and gave us a smile. All of a sudden, her sharp angular features softened and were replaced by the most jovial-looking face I'd ever seen. Her eyes were warm and her tone welcoming as she said, "Yes, that's me. Hello there, Cassia dear. And hello to you too, Stanley. It's an absolute pleasure to see you both. How kind you are to come and pay me a visit this lovely day. Come closer so I can get a good look at you both."

We didn't hesitate in moving closer, and when we came to a stop in front of Mrs Merryweather, she gave us loving looks as if we were the most important beings in the world. A warm feeling travelled all the way down my body as if someone had tipped hot chocolate down me.

Mrs Merryweather was about a foot smaller than me, and as she looked up into my eyes the love I felt coming from her intensified. She put her hand under my chin and said, "Cassia, tell me how you are. This must be a very difficult time for you; you've suddenly found yourself with a great deal of responsibility. How are you feeling about it all? Remembering you're a witch must have taken its toll on you. Tell me everything you're thinking and feeling."

I couldn't take my gaze away from her kind, probing eyes. I said, "It's okay. It's a bit of a shock, and I'm still coming to terms with it. But I know I can deal with being a witch, and with my new responsibilities. Although, I feel as if I – " I abruptly stopped. I wasn't here to talk about myself.

Mrs Merryweather nodded in understanding and released my chin. She said, "You can tell me more about it inside. Now, let me talk to this beautiful cat at your side." She hunkered down and gave her full attention to Stanley. He immediately purred.

"Now then, Stanley," Mrs Merryweather began. "How are you doing? I can see you've been through a very stressful time, and that you've done a wonderful job of keeping Cassia company all these years. That must have been such a strain on you considering that you've known all along she was a witch, and a clever witch at that. What a huge responsibility on such little shoulders. How do you feel about it all?"

Stanley purred again before saying, "It has been a very difficult time, and I've been tempted to talk to Cassia on many occasions. I've done my best, but I feel as if I've let her down." He shook his head sorrowfully and added, "I've spent many a restless night worrying about her."

Mrs Merryweather nodded in understanding. "You've been such a brave cat, Stanley. And now you've got to be even braver. How do you feel about that?"

I thought back to Gran and Oliver's comments about Mrs Merryweather, and I could now understand why people would tell her all their problems. She had a very accommodating manner about her, and she gave the impression of having all the time in the world to listen to your woes. While that was quite tempting, we didn't have time for it.

Mrs Merryweather hadn't finished with Stanley yet, and she went on, "I spoke to your brother, Oliver, recently. He's been very worried about you, and he's had many restless nights too. It took him a while to open up to me, but when he did, he told me about his concerns for himself, you and the future of witchcraft. Your brother worries an awful lot. I think another chat with me might help him. You must tell him to come and see me again soon."

"I will."

Mrs Merryweather put her hand on top of Stanley's head. "You look as if you haven't been taking care of your own needs. Tell me about that."

Before Stanley could reply, I said to Mrs Merryweather, "I'm sorry, but we don't have time to chat about ourselves. We're here to talk about Jonathan

Tidewell. My gran seems to think you might be able to help us."

Mrs Merryweather straightened up and gave me a warm smile. "Yes, Esther is right, of course. I can tell you about Jonathan." She moved over to the front door and pushed it open. "Please, do come inside and take a seat in the kitchen. I've just made some chocolate chip cookies, and there's a pan of hot chocolate simmering on the stove. I've got some delicious double cream for you, Stanley, if you would like some?"

Stanley purred once again. I'd never heard him purr so many times in a day. In fact, I hadn't heard him purr much since we moved into our apartment. That ever ready guilt over Stanley prodded me again.

Mrs Merryweather had already gone through the open door, so we had no option but to follow her. As soon as we stepped into her house, the tantalising aroma of freshly baked cookies tickled my nose. We followed the smell and headed down the hallway and into the lovely open kitchen.

Mrs Merryweather invited me to take a seat at the kitchen table. She placed a cushion on the floor for Stanley to put his bottom on. In front of the cushion was a bowl of cream. Stanley was lapping it up before I'd even sat down. Mrs Merryweather brought me a huge mug of hot chocolate which had been topped with whipped cream and sprinkles of chocolate. As if that wasn't enough, she placed a plate with cookies right in front of me. It would have been impolite of me to refuse so I immediately picked a cookie up and bit into it. They were just as delicious as they smelled.

Mrs Merryweather sat herself down opposite me and placed her hands on the table. She said, "Cassia, you enjoy your snack while I tell you what I know about Jonathan."

She didn't need to tell me twice. I pulled the hot chocolate towards me and scooped some of the whipped cream up using the spoon which Mrs Merryweather had thoughtfully placed at the side of the mug.

Mrs Merryweather said, "Jonathan Tidewell was a lovely man. Always softly spoken and extremely thoughtful. He wasn't like any of the other werewolves at all. I wasn't sure about him at first when he offered to do odd jobs for me around the house and garden, but I took stock of him, and I could see he was honest and trustworthy. He didn't prove me wrong, and I could always rely on him to do a good job around here. At first, I got the impression he wanted to kept busy so he could spend time away from his pack. Despite saying he had accepted his changed circumstances, I sensed it was difficult for him to completely accept it. Well, it would be for anyone, wouldn't it? To suddenly find yourself a werewolf, and your family slain, is not an easy thing to accept."

I nodded in agreement, and then scooped more of the delicious whipped cream into my mouth.

"Jonathan made the best out of every situation, and it wasn't long before I could see his happiness was genuine. We had many chats in this kitchen, and he told me about his increasing fondness for Anju. That fondness soon turned into love, and he was over the moon with delight." She let out a little chuckle and continued, "If that's the right expression to use for a werewolf. He was beaming with joy when he told me about their engagement. He said he was finally putting his past behind him and he was ready to move on with his life. I was so happy for him. He deserved all the happiness in the world after what had happened to his family.

"But then a few days after telling me about the engagement, his behaviour started to change. It was almost as if he was battling with his inner demons. He said he was having bad dreams which were incredibly vivid; so vivid that they felt real."

"What sort of dreams?" I asked. "I spoke to Anju earlier, and she mentioned the same thing about his dreams. But Jonathan wouldn't go into details with her about the dreams."

Mrs Merryweather gave me a knowing look. "Jonathan opened up to me. He always did. His dreams, well nightmares really, were about the night his family had been attacked. He kept having the same dreams in which he was unable to protect his family. He dreamt that he hid in a shed during the attack when he should have been outside protecting them. In his dream, Jonathan trembled in the shed whilst his wife and son were killed."

I frowned. "Did that actually happen? I knew he'd been injured but did Jonathan hide in the shed during the attack?"

Mrs Merryweather shook her head. "I spoke to Strom about this. He had a conversation with the werewolf who attacked Jonathan's family. The werewolf, Gregor, admitted that Jonathan did his best to defend his family, and he threw himself at Gregor over and over again in an attempt to hurt him. Gregor said he lashed out at Jonathan and threw him against a wall. Jonathan blacked out, and Gregor thought he was dead. This evil werewolf then attacked Jonathan's wife and son, and there was nothing Jonathan could have done to prevent it. Thankfully, Strom disposed of Gregor before he could ever attack again."

I asked, "Did Jonathan know the truth about what had happened?"

"He did. I told him, and Strom told him too. But the dreams Jonathan was having kept interfering with reality. He believed the dreams were more real than what Strom and I were telling him."

I frowned. "That doesn't make any sense at all. Do you think Jonathan felt so guilty about being happy that he brought those dreams upon himself?"

"That is entirely possible. But you would expect the dreams to go away after a while, especially with all the reassuring talks Strom and I were having with Jonathan. That wasn't the case. The dreams increased in intensity, and the details became more real. He was plagued by his nightmares and could barely function."

"When did you last see Jonathan alive?"

"It was on the morning he died. I was on my way to the market and was in a hurry because the fresh bread soon sells out there. I caught a glimpse of Jonathan as he was fixing somebody's fence. He'd received a butterfly message. It was one of those messages which was written on the butterfly's wings. I saw its wings opening and Jonathan reading the message. He had his back to me, and I didn't see his expression. Like I said, I was in a rush to get to the market, and I didn't stop to observe anything further. We get messages all the time around here, so it didn't strike me as an unusual occurrence." She sighed heavily. "Of course, now I know different, and I realise that message could have been important."

I asked, "Is it possible to find out what the message said? Would the butterfly who delivered the message remember it?"

Mrs Merryweather gave me a puzzled look. "How much witch training have you had since coming back here?"

"Not much; barely anything. I'm relying on my common sense; what there is of that."

"Don't put yourself down, Cassia. You're doing a marvellous job. I can feel the strength and courage in you. The reason why I'm asking about how much training you've had is because there's a spell you could use on the butterflies to find out which one took the message to Jonathan. You might even be able to find out what the message was. I think it's a spell which involves the essence of the memory of the butterfly in question. Esther would know more about it. You should speak to her about it. Would you like some more hot chocolate? You soon finished that one."

I looked down in surprise at my empty mug. I hadn't realised I'd drunk it so quickly. "No, thank you. We'd better be going. We've got work to do."

Mrs Merryweather laid a hand on top of mine and said, "Are you sure? I feel like you have a great burden on your shoulders, and it would be a comfort to you if you told me what those burdens where. I'm an extremely good listener, and I've got nothing else to do today but listen to you." She gave me the kindest of smiles, and I was so tempted to stay in that lovely kitchen with delicious hot chocolate all day and to spill my every care and concern out to her.

Reluctantly, I pulled my hand from beneath hers and forced myself to stand up. "No, thank you again. It's been great to meet you. Thank you for the information about Jonathan. We really must get going."

I turned around and looked at Stanley. He was fast asleep on the cushion with his eyes closed and was snoring gently. Bits of cream were dabbed around his mouth and on his whiskers.

Mrs Merryweather stood up and said, "You can leave Stanley here with me if you like. I could have a good chat with him. It would do him the world of good to talk about what's been troubling him these last few months. Poor little thing."

Again, I was tempted to do as she asked. But no, Stanley was my cat, and he was coming with me, whether he liked it or not. I said thank you again to Mrs Merryweather for her kind offer, then I strode over to Stanley, picked him up and tucked him under my arm. I strode purposefully out of Mrs Merryweather's enchanted cottage.

It was time for me to perform my first magic spell.

Chapter 23

We headed back across Brimstone town square, and as we did so, I could feel heads turning to watch us.

I said to Stanley, "We've been back and forth across this town square all day. We're not very professional are we? I bet Gran and Oliver don't do this back-and-forth thing. They probably find their suspects immediately, and get to work with their investigation. Everyone is watching us and probably wondering what we're doing. I feel such a twit."

Stanley said, "We're still new to this business. I'm sure we'll get the hang of it soon. Don't pay any attention to anyone else's opinions."

"I'll try."

I tried not to care as we were blatantly gawped at as we hastened across the square, but it was more difficult to ignore the pointing and the sound of laughing. How rude.

As we headed past the butterfly tree on the cobbled road, I gave it a quick inspection and saw the butterflies were in the very same position as they had been earlier with their wings closed.

I said to Stanley, "If I'm to take on the memories of one of the butterflies, how will I know which one to focus on?"

"I've no idea. Let's leave that to your gran to sort out."

We hurried through the cellar door, and I was relieved to close it behind us. I'm sure I could hear jeering now.

We found Gran in the kitchen, thankfully nearer the floor than the ceiling this time. She was sitting at the table doing a crossword puzzle. I sat opposite her and told her what Mrs Merryweather had said. Stanley jumped onto my knee and added the bit about him lapping up the double cream.

Gran gave me a sharp look when I mentioned the spell for the butterfly. She said, "Mrs Merryweather shouldn't have mentioned that to you. It's a dangerous spell, and it's only for witches with advanced education."

"Why is it dangerous?"

Gran explained, "When you take on someone's memories, they could be highly painful memories which could implant themselves into your brain. You would then think the memories are part of you. I've known this happen to witches and it changed their lives entirely. And not for the better. The other thing is that you could take on the physical attributions of the creature you're connecting with. Cassia, you could turn into a butterfly forever, and there would be nothing I could do about it."

I considered the matter. "Being a butterfly wouldn't be such a bad thing. I wouldn't have to worry about paying my mortgage."

Gran said, "Don't be flippant about it. I've seen this happen more than once, and it's not something I want to happen to you. I prefer you as you are."

I wouldn't let the matter drop and continued, "You're an experienced witch. If you were at my side guiding me through the spell, would it work?"

Gran hesitated. "We could do a weaker spell, but there's still an element of danger. The good thing about the Brimstone butterflies is that they have a collective consciousness and we wouldn't have to use the actual butterfly who delivered the message to Jonathan. One of the other butterflies could have a weaker memory of that incident." She tapped the kitchen table while she thought about it. "Yes, we could do that. Henry would be the best butterfly to use."

"Henry? I didn't know the butterflies had names."

"Of course they've got names. Why wouldn't they? Henry is the butterfly I use most often to deliver my messages. I suspect he's the one who came to your office that day to let you know I'd been injured. He must have been nearby when I called out for help and recorded my voice. He's highly intelligent. Goodness knows how he found his way to your office." She called out for Oliver.

Oliver came into the kitchen, looked at Gran and said, "You called?"

Gran said, "Oliver, can you go and collect Henry for me, please? Take Stanley with you. Show him how to beckon the butterflies. It will be good training for him."

Oliver gave her a nod and said, "Will do." He looked over Stanley and made a beckoning motion with his head. Stanley leapt off my knee and followed Oliver out of the kitchen

I said to Gran, "Do I need to open the cellar door for them?"

"There's no need. There's a cat flap in the door. Didn't you notice it?"

I shook my head. "No, but it does make sense to have one. What do we do now? How do we prepare for my first ever spell?"

"You can put the kettle on."

"Ooo. Is there a special potion I need to mix with hot water? How exciting." I stood up.

Gran shook her head. "No, I'd like a coffee and I can't be bothered doing it myself. Make yourself one too. You could do with a caffeine boost. You'll have to keep your wits about you when we do this spell."

"Right. Okay."

I busied myself with making hot drinks for Gran and me. By the time the drinks were ready, Oliver and Stanley had returned to the kitchen. A pale yellow butterfly was resting on Oliver's back.

Oliver said, "I've explained the situation to Henry, and he's happy to help."

Gran gave the butterfly a kind smile and said, "Thank you, Henry." She looked at me. "Take a big drink of coffee while I get the spell ready in my mind. I haven't used this spell recently, and it's going to take me a minute or two to search for the right words." She tapped the side of her head. "The words are in here somewhere. Hopefully."

I concentrated on drinking as much coffee as I could while Gran mumbled incoherently to herself. I tried to swallow my nervousness with the coffee. Was this a good idea? Then I thought about the kind things everyone had said about Jonathan. I had to help him in some way. If he had been murdered, I wanted to find out who had done it.

Gran slapped her hand on the table and declared, "I think I've remembered all the words now. Right, let's begin."

She looked towards Henry who was still resting on Oliver's back. She gave him a nod and said, "Henry, fly over to Cassia." Gran looked back at me and said, "Open your left hand and keep it steady."

I did so, and watched as Henry flew over to me. He landed gently in my hand. I could barely feel his weight.

I said to Gran, "Now what?"

"Close your eyes and clear your mind. Hopefully, the memories of the butterfly who delivered the message to Jonathan will come to your mind through Henry. Don't fight it."

I gave her a small nod. I closed my eyes and tried to clear my mind. It wasn't that easy to do considering Gran's spell might go wrong and that I might turn into a butterfly forever.

I took some deep breaths and concentrated on clearing the thoughts one by one from my mind. I felt a slight pressure on my left palm and wondered what Henry was doing to me. Was he giving me a butterfly kiss?

I took more deep breaths and slowly, very slowly, a different feeling came over me. In my mind's eye I see myself flying above Brimstone town square. I wasn't at all scared, and it felt like a joyful experience. I flew right over the square and towards the forest. The tops of the trees looked amazing from this height. I carried on flying and went past the big oak tree where Jonathan had met his end. I carried on, knowing exactly where I was headed. I saw a man in the distance near a fence, and I knew it was Jonathan Tidewell.

As I came closer, he turned around and saw me. He smiled at me and held his hand out. I landed on his open palm. There was a twitchy feeling on my back which I assumed was the written message appearing on my wings.

I heard Jonathan say, 'They want to meet me at the oak tree? Okay, tell them I'll be there in ten minutes. Thank you for the message.'

I felt the twitch of my wings again as I lifted off his palm. I flew back over the trees. As I did so, the name 'Sarah' came to my mind. Who was Sarah? The butterfly who'd delivered the message to Jonathan? Or the being who had sent the message to him?

I continued soaring above the trees and then started to head down. Someone was beckoning me, but I couldn't see who it was, I just had a feeling I was needed.

Downwards I went. All of a sudden, something was flung over me which dragged me to the ground. A net? My heart sped up, and terror shot through me. I could hear a mumbled voice, but I couldn't work out where it was coming from or what they were saying. The world went dark around me, and my heart was beating so fast I thought it was going to burst.

The next thing I could sense was being somewhere completely dark. I felt resistance as I tried to open my wings. It was soon obvious I was trapped somewhere. I tried to catch my breath, but it was getting harder and harder for me to breathe. I blinked into the darkness. Where was I? Panic rose in me, and I felt as if I was going to stop breathing at any second.

I could hear someone shouting 'Cassia' over and over again. Then I felt a sharp prod on my arm. My eyes sprang open, and I saw the concerned face of Gran who was now shaking me roughly.

Gran shouted, "Cassia! Breathe! Please!" She slapped me on the cheek and shouted again, "Breathe! Cassia!"

My right hand clawed at my throat and I gasped, "I can't! I can't breathe!"

Gran put her hands on the side of my face and looked straight into my eyes. "Cassia, take a big deep breath like me." She proceeded to inhale deeply, and I tried to do the same. It was another minute before I was breathing normally.

I looked down at my left palm and said, "Henry? Where did he go?"

Gran explained, "As soon as I saw you in distress, I asked him to fly over to Oliver's back. What happened to you? You were gasping for breath, and I could see sheer terror on your face."

I took a sip of the coffee which was now cold before telling Gran and the cats what had happened. I looked at Henry and noticed his yellow wings were firmly closed.

"Gran, what does this all mean? And who is Sarah?"

Gran said, "We'll ask Henry. He can't talk, but he can indicate yes or no with his wings." She turned to face Henry and said, "Who is Sarah? Is she the butterfly who delivered the message to Jonathan?"

Henry slowly opened his wings and flapped them twice.

Gran explained, "Cassia, that means yes. One flap of his wings is no." She carried on talking to Henry. "Has Sarah returned to the butterfly tree?"

Henry flapped his wings once.

The butterflies strange behaviour suddenly made sense to me. I said to Henry, "Is Sarah lost somewhere?"

Two flaps of his wings. Yes.

I continued, "Have all the Brimstone butterflies been looking for her?"

Yes.

I hesitantly asked my next question, "Is Sarah still alive?"

Yes.

"If she lost somewhere? Perhaps trapped somewhere?" I asked.

Yes

Gran said, "Poor Sarah. The butterflies must be feeling her fear and despair. That must be why they all disappeared recently; they were out looking for her. Whoever has trapped her is an evil, evil creature, and we must do our best to find Sarah immediately."

I nodded. "It's obvious that whoever captured Sarah has something to do with Jonathan's death. Gran, this is awful. What can I do about it?"

"You have to go back to Brimstone and be more forceful with your questions. There is evil lurking in the town; the kind of evil that has never been there before. Murdering a werewolf is bad enough, but trapping one of the town's beautiful butterflies is beyond belief." Gran put her hand over her mouth to stifle a yawn. "I'll come with you. I'll need to take a couple of painkillers before I do. This stupid ankle is bothering me again."

I got to my feet. "You're not in a fit state to help me. Gran, you need to go back to bed and rest. I can deal with this."

Gran looked as if she was about to argue with me, so I said more insistently, "Gran, if I'm going to be a witch and help you, I need all the experience I can get. This is something I want to do. And I'll have Stanley with me. You have to trust me."

Gran gave me a helpless shrug. "It doesn't look like I have much choice, does it? Can you help me upstairs? I've still got a bit of levitation potion in me so I should be able to float most of the way. Cassia, I'm still not sure about this, but I can see the determination in your eyes."

Oliver said, "We'd better take Henry back to the tree. Stanley, you come with me again."

The cats left the kitchen, and I managed to manoeuvre Gran upstairs and into bed. I put the book paperweights at the corners of the bed cover again, just in case. I gave Gran the painkillers that Dr Gilbert had prescribed. I didn't know what was in them, but they were certainly strong as Gran was asleep within a minute.

I went downstairs and into the living room to wait for the return of the cats. I paced about the living room and thought about what I was going to do next. I really didn't have any idea at all and kept waiting for inspiration to strike me. It was taking its time.

As I continued to pace, the sun shone through the window and landed on something which stopped me in my tracks. There was something catching the sunlight on the back of the sofa. I moved closer to inspect it. I saw a couple of strands of long hair lying across the sofa. I carefully picked them up and held them up to the light. The strands of hair were of a burnished copper colour.

Anju.

She must have been in this room. The only reason she could have been in here was to carry Gran back from Brimstone following her attack. My jaw clenched in anger. Why hadn't she told me the second I met her? Had she sent the butterfly message to Jonathan and then murdered him? Had she attacked Gran in the hope of killing her too? Or was she covering up for the one who was guilty? Strom? Flint? Were the werewolves all covering up for each other?

When Oliver and Stanley padded into the room, I said, "Stanley, we're going back to Brimstone and we're going to face that evil, conniving pack of werewolves."

Chapter 24

I was furious as I headed back across Brimstone town square. I didn't care that everyone was turning to watch Stanley and me as we stormed along. How dare Anju not tell me about Gran?

I was still mad as I headed towards the werewolf village. My anger kept me going as I walked over to the first man I encountered in the werewolf village.

I jabbed him on the shoulder and demanded, "Where is Anju? Is she here somewhere?"

"What's it got to do with you, witch? Your sort is unwelcome around here. Clear off if you know what's good for you."

I jabbed him again on his shoulder, briefly noticing how hard his muscles were. "I need to talk to Anju right now. Do you know where she is or not?"

The man snarled, "Jab me once more, and I'll bite your fingers off."

"Oh yeah? Just try it." The sensible part of my brain was trying to get through to me and was telling me to stop arguing with a big werewolf, but I ignored it.

Stanley curled around my legs and called up, "Cassia, I can see Anju going into that cabin over there."

I glanced over to where Stanley was looking, and I saw Anju walking into a cabin a short distance away. I turned back to the man in front of me and attempted to give him a disparaging look. "Luckily for you, I have to go now."

He sneered, "Yeah, lucky for me."

With Stanley at my side, I walked over to the cabin Anju had entered and knocked on the door. She answered it, and I blurted out, "You've been in Gran's house! I found your hair there! Why didn't you tell me you'd been there?"

Anju blanched, and her hands shot to her chest. In a quiet voice, she said, "You'd better come in. I can explain everything."

I followed her into the cabin, and even though I was still feeling angry, I took a moment to appreciate the cosiness of the interior. All the furniture had been made out of wood, and there were comfy-looking cushions everywhere. A welcoming log fire was burning in a hearth at the far side of the room. It was all very homely and welcoming. But I wasn't in the mood to feel welcomed; I was in the mood to vent my anger over Gran's attack.

Anju indicated for us to take a seat. We went over to the large sofa and sat down. It was incredibly soft, and I felt myself sinking into the cushions.

Anju took a seat opposite us, and before I could say a word, she broke down and started to cry. My eyes narrowed. She'd cried in front of me before. I wasn't going to be fooled by her crocodile tears again.

She said, "Yes, it was me who took your gran back home. But I didn't have anything to do with her injuries. I promise. I would never do that to Esther. Never. Please, you have to believe me."

I studied her for a moment. I could feel the genuine remorse coming from her. All my anger vanished, and I shuffled along the sofa until I was able to pat her on the arm.

When Anju had composed herself, she said, "I was near the oak tree when Esther was injured. I heard a cry of pain, and when I went to investigate, I found her unconscious on the ground. I couldn't leave her there, so I picked her up and took her to her house. I used the back paths to get to the door so that I wasn't seen by anyone in Brimstone. Jonathan had spoken to me many

153

times about his human life, and I knew how much you humans rely on doctors. I knew that's what I had to do for Esther. I put her on the sofa and soon found the doctor's telephone number." She gave me a wry smile. "I've never used a telephone before, and it took me a while to work out what to do. I waited at Esther's side until the doctor arrived. I'm so sorry I didn't tell you this earlier."

"Why didn't you tell me?"

"It's illegal for me to enter your world. If Blythe had found out, I could have been sent away from my pack." She gave me a searching look. "Cassia, it wasn't me who hurt Esther. Honest."

I wasn't sure I fully believed Anju's story yet. She did seem genuine, but that could mean she was an expert liar. I couldn't quite read her feelings.

I said, "Do you have something else to tell me about that day? I spoke to Gran, and she told me she saw you and Flint canoodling by the oak tree."

Anju frowned. "Canoodling? We weren't canoodling, whatever that is. Flint was trying to comfort me. I'd gone to the oak tree to think about Jonathan. Flint found me there and took it upon himself to comfort me. It wasn't long before he started saying horrible things about Jonathan and how he'd never been part of our werewolf pack. I politely told him to keep his thoughts to himself, but he wouldn't listen. He went on and on about how it was a blessing that Jonathan had gone and that I could be with someone of my own kind. I couldn't take his despicable words anymore and I ordered him to leave. He went running off, and it was a few minutes later that I heard your gran yell." A look of surprise came onto her face. "Flint! It could have been Flint who attacked Esther. He was in a terrible mood when he ran away. Would he do that to her?"

Stanley and I nodded at the same time.

"I never hurt the old crone!" Flint stormed into the room and jabbed his finger in my direction. "I never hurt the interfering old crone."

Anju shot to her feet and yelled, "Flint, how many times have I told you? You do not enter my home uninvited. Stop shouting at my guests and get out immediately." Her hands were clenched into fists at her side.

Flint took a step back and said, "You need protecting, Anju. You need me. When are you going to admit it?"

A yellow fire flashed in Anju's eyes and her hands clenched even more. In a low voice she said, "Flint, this is the last time I'm going to tell you. I do not need you in my life. I do not want you hanging around me. And I certainly don't want you barging into my home. One more incident like this and I'll be having a word with my father. We might have to take drastic action concerning your future in our pack. Am I making myself clear?"

Flint swallowed and took another step back. In a subdued tone he said, "Yes, I'm sorry. I understand." His shoulders dropped and he looked in my direction. "It wasn't me who attacked your gran. That's the truth."

I nodded, but I didn't believe him for a second. I said, "You followed me the other day after I spoke to Strom. You followed me along the forest path. Why?"

He shrugged. "I wanted to make sure you got back to the town safely."

I shook my head. He was lying. I had another question for him. "You were heard arguing with Jonathan on the morning he died. What were you arguing about?"

Confusion crossed Flint's features. "I wasn't arguing with him. It was impossible to argue with Jonathan. He was too polite, too mealy-mouthed, too human. There wasn't one ounce of werewolf in him."

Anju stamped her foot on the ground. "Enough is enough!" She shouted. "Flint, get out now!"

Flint lowered his head and left the room without uttering another word.

Anju turned her blazing eyes in our direction and said, "I think it's time you left. I don't want to talk about Jonathan anymore. I want to be alone to grieve about him."

I wanted to ask more questions, but my attention was drawn to her hands which were dangling at her side. Was it my imagination or were her fingernails slowly growing into talons? Was she changing into a werewolf in front of me?

I quickly stood up. I wasn't staying here to find out. I picked Stanley up and put him under my arm. I said goodbye and thank you to Anju and then swiftly left the cabin.

As we quickly made our way away from the cabin, Stanley whispered, "Cassia, did you see her fingernails? Was she changing into a werewolf?"

I gave him a brief nod. "We have to get away from here. I don't feel safe."

We continued to hasten forward. I could have sworn I heard growling behind me, but that could have been my imagination going into overdrive.

As soon as we hit the path, I broke into a jog.

Stanley was still tucked under my arm, and he hissed, "Cassia, there's someone following us. I can smell them. They smell like a wet dog."

I hear someone behind us too. I started to run. I always seemed to be running away from something around these parts.

There was a sudden loud growl, and I yelped in surprise.

Stanley jumped to the ground and turned around to face whatever was following us. "Cassia! It's a werewolf! It's heading this way."

My legs took that moment to decide they'd had enough of running and came to a sudden stop.

Stanley said, "I'll deal with it. I'll protect you."

I slowly turned around to face the creature. I couldn't leave little Stanley to cope with a wild beast on his own.

I forgot to breathe as I saw a huge wolf walking towards us. It had bright yellow eyes, and its lips were pulled back to reveal large, sharp teeth.

Stanley darted forward and shouted, "Back off! I won't let you hurt my Cassia!"

The wolf leapt forward, lashed out at Stanley and sent him flying into the bushes.

"Stanley!" I cried out.

The wolf looked my way, saliva dripped from its teeth. I watched in slow motion as the wolf came closer.

Chapter 25

I closed my eyes and waited for death to arrive. A little thought flashed into my mind about how unusual it was to be killed by a werewolf. I wondered if that would be stated as my cause of demise on my death certificate. Would it be carved on my headstone? Would a notice go online? Probably not. Gran would have to make something up about how I died. Shame. Death by werewolf would have been impressive.

As more thoughts gathered momentum, I realised death hadn't arrived yet. If that werewolf was going to kill me, I wish it would hurry up and get on with it. I didn't have all day.

I carefully opened one eye and looked at the creature in front of me. A huge shadow had fallen over the werewolf, and it was looking skywards and trembling. I opened my other eye. I could make out the shape of the shadow which was covering the werewolf and a lot of the area behind it. It was paw shaped. I looked up to where the werewolf was staring and could see an enormous paw raised in the air. It was twice the size of a bus.

The ground shook as a voice boomed out, "Leave! Now!"

The werewolf whimpered, turned around and scampered away.

My knees suddenly buckled, and I collapsed to the ground. I knew any immediate danger had passed as I recognised the booming voice. It was Luca's. I looked up again and could just about see his rabbit face. He looked as if he were about a hundred feet away.

He waved his paw at me and said, "Hello."

Luca shrank to a normal sized bunny and then changed into his human form. He put his hands out and helped me to my feet.

He said, "Cassia, are you alright? Did that werewolf hurt you?"

I wiped the dirt from my behind and answered, "No, I'm alright, thank you. You turned up in the nick of time. Were you going to squash that werewolf?"

"If I had to, I would have done. Are you sure you're okay?"

"Stanley!" I cried out. "Stanley was flung into the bushes. Where is he?"

"I'm here," said a familiar voice. Stanley came through the bushes, looking a little bit worse for wear, but all in one piece. He looked over at Luca and said, "Luca! I haven't seen you since you were a little boy."

Stanley scampered over to Luca and wound himself in and out of Luca's legs.

Luca laughed, bent over and tickled Stanley affectionately behind his ears. "Now then, Stanley. How are you, my friend?"

"All the better for seeing you. Was that enormous rabbit you?"

Luca nodded. "Yes. I know I'm not a ferocious-looking creature, but I didn't have time to change into one. Still, becoming enormous did the trick, and the werewolf has gone now."

I wagged my finger between Luca and Stanley. "How do you two know each other?"

They both gave me the same incredulous look. Stanley said, "We used to play together when you and Luca were young. Don't you remember?"

I shook my head sadly. "I can't remember everything yet. Perhaps I will soon."

Luca asked again, "Cassia, are you sure you're alright?"

"Apart from thinking I was going to be mauled to death by a werewolf, yes, I'm alright. What are you doing in this part of the forest? Are you working?"

Luca ran a hand through his thick hair and said, "I was on patrol in another part of the forest. I had a feeling that something was wrong over here, and I was right. When I came over to this area, I could hear someone following you. I was just about to show myself in human form when the werewolf leapt towards you. I knew my human form wouldn't scare it, so I quickly increased in size. That worked." He gave me a small grin.

I looked back along the path and said, "Luca, did you see who the werewolf was? Did you see them before they changed into a werewolf?"

He shook his head. "Unfortunately not. But I'll find out, don't you worry about that. There's something weird going on in this forest lately. First, your gran was attacked, and now someone's gone after you. I don't like this at all. Cassia, what are you doing in this part of the forest anyway?"

"I'm still looking into the death of Jonathan Tidewell." I remembered how I'd spoken to Luca the last time we'd met. I added, "I'm sorry for being so rude to you when you offered your help to me. I wish I'd taken you up on your offer. I've no idea what I'm doing."

Luca gave me a broad grin. "That's okay. I could try and help you now if you like? You can talk to me about what investigations you've made so far. I've seen you and Stanley walking to and fro across the town square. Do you want to tell me what's been going on?"

"I would love to, thank you."

Luca said, "Why don't we head back into town? I don't want to take the chance of that werewolf sneaking up on us."

"Good idea." I turned in the direction of the path that led back to Brimstone.

Luca looked down at Stanley and said, "You look tired, my friend. Would you like a lift back to town?"

Stanley replied, "Yes, please. I am a bit winded by my tumble in the bushes."

Luca picked Stanley up and snuggled him next to his chest.

A purring noise came from Stanley, and he said to me, "Cassia, look how strong Luca's arms are. Hasn't he got strong arms?"

I nodded and averted my gaze from Luca's impressive-looking arms.

Stanley went on, "Look at his broad chest. Hasn't he got a lovely broad chest?"

I nodded again and concentrated on the path in front of me.

Stanley hadn't finished. "Cassia, have you noticed how handsome Luca is? Look at his beautiful blue eyes. Haven't you've got a pendant that colour? Isn't it your favourite pendant?"

My cheeks warmed up, and I concentrated even more on the path in front of me.

I swiftly changed the subject and said to Luca, "I've been talking to Mrs Merryweather about Jonathan, and she said he was having terrible dreams. Luca, is it possible for someone to put nightmares in someone else's head by the power of suggestion?"

Luca replied, "It certainly is. And it would be easy to do so if they used black magic. That's not something that's used in Brimstone, though."

"Let's just say that someone was using it. Where would they get black magic from? Or is it something you learn how to do?"

"Someone would need to go looking for it, and it comes in various forms. Why are you asking? Do you think black magic was used on Jonathan?"

I frowned. "I don't know. I'm still new to all this magic business. I also spoke to Tansy, and she told me she heard Flint arguing with Jonathan shortly before his death. Do you think Flint is capable of hurting Jonathan?"

Luca said, "Last week I would have said no, but I don't know what's got into the werewolves lately. When you say arguing, what do you mean?"

"Tansy said they were both shouting."

"That's impossible. Jonathan wasn't capable of shouting. When he was originally attacked by a werewolf, Jonathan's vocal chords were partly ripped open. He could barely talk above a whisper, even in his werewolf form."

We came to the edge of the town square. Certain residents were rushing about and calling to each other.

"What's going on?" I asked.

Luca said, "I'm not sure. Those are guardians. It looks as if they're heading towards Blythe's house."

One of the guardians, a young woman, looked over our way and called out, "Luca, there's an urgent meeting. Hurry up."

Luca put Stanley on the ground and said to me, "I have to go. Will you be okay getting back to your house?"

I nodded.

Luca flashed me a smile before hurrying away.

We watched him go, and when he'd disappeared from sight, I turned around and headed back into the forest.

Stanley ran at my side and said, "Where are we going? I thought we were going home."

I looked down at my friend and said, "I think I know who killed Jonathan Tidewell."

Chapter 26

I headed straight over to Tansy's house with Stanley jogging at my side. I opened the small garden gate and walked along the path to her front door.

Stanley said, "Why are we here?"

"Tansy lied to me about hearing Jonathan and Flint shouting at each other. I want to know what else she lied about." I raised my hand and knocked on the wooden door.

Stanley suddenly arched his back and made a loud, hissing noise.

His back flattened out, and he looked up at me and said, "I'm so sorry for swearing like that. I don't know what came over me." His whiskers twitched as he looked left and right. "There's something evil around here, I can sense it."

I knocked again on the door and waited. There was still no answer. I reached out and opened the door, stuck my head through and called out for Tansy. There was no reply.

Stanley said, "We should leave, right now."

"Now that we're here, we may as well see if Tansy is inside somewhere. I want to have another talk with her. I've got a funny feeling about her."

Before Stanley could convince me otherwise, I stepped into the house. I continued to call out Tansy's name, but there was no answering reply.

I walked into the kitchen and looked around at the shelves and work surfaces.

Stanley said, "What are you looking for?"

I shrugged. "Lotions and potions? A spell book? A list of black magic incantations? I've no idea. Can you pick up on anything in here?"

Stanley put his nose to the wooden floor and began to sniff. He moved along the floor continuing to sniff as he did so. He came to a stop further along and looked back at me. "There's a trapdoor here, Cassia."

I went over to where Stanley was and looked down at the trapdoor.

"A trapdoor," I said. "It would be a trapdoor, wouldn't it? There's always a trapdoor in horror movies and on TV shows. And you know full well there's going to be something horrendous waiting for our hero beneath the trapdoor."

Stanley said, "Why don't we walk out of here right now? We can come back another time to question Tansy. I don't like it here. Something's not right."

"I feel the same, but we have to do do this. Stand back, and I'll open the dreaded trapdoor."

I put my hand on the metal ring of the door and lifted it. "You stay here, and I'll go down and investigate."

"No way. We're a team." Before I could stop him, he scampered down the wooden steps beneath the open trapdoor.

I whipped out my phone and put the torch on. I shone it down into the darkness and saw Stanley a few steps down. He moved his head left and right as I aimed the torch towards the bottom of the steps.

He said, "I can't see any corpses or hideous weapons of torture. I can see a light pulley, though. Just a moment." He ran down the rest of the steps, and a moment later the area beneath the trapdoor flooded with light.

I carefully lowered myself to the first step and called out, "Stanley? Are you alright down there?"

"Yes, there's a big room down here. You'd better come down and have a look at this."

I went down the next few steps, closed the trapdoor behind me, and then slowly descended the rest of the steps.

Stanley was standing in front of a wall which was covered in drawings of Jonathan Tidewell. There were images of Jonathan in various poses, and in different places. Jonathan fixing the roof tiles on Tansy's house, Jonathan in the garden leaning against a fence. Jonathan sitting on a picnic blanket on the grass waving a sandwich in the air. It was like looking at the wall of a serial stalker. Or a murderer.

I stated the obvious, "Tansy was obsessed with him."

My attention was drawn to a different kind of image at the side of the others. It showed a werewolf with their head chopped off. The werewolf had long, copper coloured hair. Obviously Anju.

Stanley looked at me. "It seems Tansy was in love with Jonathan. She must have been outraged when he got engaged to Anju. Do you think she killed him?"

"She's only little, so if she did kill him, she must have used magic of some sort. See if you can find any evidence of magic in here. Perhaps any bottles or spells. Anything that looks suspicious."

Stanley nodded and then began to investigate.

I looked along the nearest table and was drawn to a small, wooden box. I had a feeling I knew what, or who was inside.

I lifted the lid of the box, and my heart sank as I saw a green butterfly lying on the bottom of the box. I whispered, "Sarah? Is that you?"

Stanley jumped onto the table and came over to the box. He peered inside and said quietly, "Is she dead?"

"I don't know. I hope not." I carefully put my hand inside the box and lifted the butterfly out. She lay flat on my hand. I could feel the tiniest of heartbeats and said to Stanley, "I think she's still alive, but only just."

Stanley looked into my eyes and said, "You have to do magic on her. Can you do that?"

"I can try, but I don't really know what I'm doing."

"I think you do, Cassia. Try."

I concentrated on the little creature. I pictured her being well again and flying above the forest. I felt a familiar tingle running through my hand, and I continued to concentrate on the feeling of Sarah flying again.

In a hushed whisper, Stanley said, "It's working. Her wings are moving."

The little butterfly slowly flapped her wings and lifted off my hands. The flapping of her wings increased, and she rose even more.

"Cassia, you did it! You did magic. I knew you could do it."

We both jumped as a cold voice behind us said, "It's not only witches who can do magic."

We spun around and saw Tansy standing halfway down the wooden steps. The hate on her face made me shiver.

She raised her hands in our direction and shouted, "Bind!"

Coils of rope shot off the nearby wall and headed towards us. A thick piece of rope wrapped itself round and round my body and then bound itself into a knot. The same thing happened to Stanley. Lengths of cloth flew our way and quickly wound themselves around our mouths.

Tansy laughed and came further down the steps. "That should keep you quiet and still for a while." She jumped as the butterfly suddenly flew past her and through the open trapdoor. Tansy hissed, "You idiots! Why did you let her go? Now I'll have to capture her again."

She came down to the bottom of the stairs and walked over to us. There was a look of intense loathing on her face as she looked us up and down.

She indicated her head in the direction of the drawings. "You found my artwork. Wasn't Jonathan a beautiful specimen? He loved me, did you know that? He was always coming to my house asking for work to do. It was so obvious how he felt about me. His feelings for Anju were false, I knew that. She forced him to get engaged. He was too polite to refuse." She smirked. "I suppose you want to know how I killed him. Fair enough, I'll tell you."

She put her hands behind her back and began to walk up and down in front of us. She began, "It was me who gave him those vivid nightmares. Whenever I made him a cup of tea, I would put a magic potion in it which made him sleepy. As he dozed, he became susceptible to my graphic descriptions of the nightmares I placed in his mind. It was amazingly easy to do. I quite enjoyed going into detail about that werewolf who bit him. I wanted him to hate all the werewolves. I wanted him to walk away from them and come and live with me. He'd be safe here with me. I would look after him forever."

Tansy stopped pacing. "But that part of my plan about Jonathan confiding in me backfired when he went to see that nosy Mrs Merryweather. He told all his problems to her instead of me. He was supposed to confide in me so that I became indispensable to him. That stupid goblin was starting to talk sense into him. He began to realise the nightmares weren't real." She shook her head in annoyance. "I'm going to make her pay for what she did."

I tried to struggle against my ropes, but doing so made them cut into my skin.

Tansy looked at the drawings behind us before saying, "I had to do something before Jonathan went ahead with those ridiculous wedding plans. I wasn't prepared to see him married to that hideous Anju. Not when he could have been with me.

"One day, when he was working in my garden, I declared my true feelings to him. I thought he would say he felt the same way and always had done. But he lied. He said he didn't love me and that his heart was with Anju. He said he was going to make a new life with her. I tried to convince him otherwise, but he wouldn't listen to me. He said it would be better if he never came back to my house. I knew Anju had twisted his mind against me." Her face twisted in bitterness. "I didn't want to kill him, but I had to. I couldn't bear the thought of him being with Anju and not me.

"I sent a butterfly message to Jonathan and made it look like it was from Anju. I asked him to meet me at the oak tree to discuss our wedding plans. When he turned up there, he was surprised to see me and immediately tried to leave. He wasn't prepared for the magic that I used on him. To be fair, I did give him one last chance to declare his love for me, but he wouldn't admit it." She shrugged. "I had no choice. He tried to struggle as I made him climb the tree, but my magic was much stronger than his will. He was still struggling as I made him tie the rope around his neck. His struggle didn't last that long. As he took his last breath, I told him he shouldn't have refused my love. It was all his fault that I had to end his life.

"I had everything in place so that Flint would get the blame for Jonathan's death. I had Flint's nightmares planned out, and I was going to convince him that he had killed Jonathan. I was going to convince Flint to murder Anju. But then you came along, Cassia Winter, and started to interfere in everything. Now I'll have to change Flint's nightmares. They'll have to include killing you and your stupid cat."

Tansy moved closer to Stanley and said, "I'll kill the cat first. I hate cats." She reached out a hand and pinched Stanley's back. His eyes widened in pain.

Hate flared up in me, and I struggled against the tight ropes again.

Tansy grabbed Stanley's tail and pulled it roughly. Stanley choked against the cloth in his mouth.

My body was seething with hate, but I knew if I was going to do magic, I would need to stay calm. I ignored the taunts Tansy was giving Stanley, and I closed my eyes. I imagined Stanley and me being free from our ropes and Tansy being the one who was tied up instead. My fingertips began to tingle, and I concentrated on the feeling of being free even more.

There was a sudden flash of light and screams came from Tansy. I was blinded by the light at first, but when I could see again I saw the ropes around Stanley and me had fallen to the floor, along with the cloths from our mouths.

I quickly scanned the room for signs of Tansy. There she was, near the steps. She was lying on the floor, bound by ropes. Her head was at a funny angle, and there was a dark liquid pooling under her head.

Stanley came over to me and said in a shocked voice, "Is she dead? Have you killed her?"

Chapter 27

"Well?" Gran asked later on. "Did you kill her?"

I was sitting in the chair at the side of Gran's bed. Stanley and Oliver were lying at the bottom of the bed facing us.

Gran sat up straighter in bed. "I'm presuming you didn't or else you wouldn't be here. I hope you at least caused her some physical damage. What a nasty little elf!"

"To be honest, Gran, I can't remember clearly what happened after Tansy was flung across the room. Blythe suddenly came dashing down the steps along with some other people. Blythe took in the situation immediately and went over to Tansy. She said she wasn't going to allow Tansy to die, not before Blythe got a full confession out of her."

I took a sip of tea. My hands were still trembling from recent events, but I tried not to show it.

Stanley took up the story. "Luca was with Blythe. He ran right over to Cassia and wrapped his strong arms around her. Cassia, hasn't Luca got strong arms?"

I nodded, and pulled my cup closer. I could feel Gran looking my way.

"I left Cassia and Luca to have a hug," Stanley said, "and I went over to Blythe. She was talking quietly to those people she was with. Blythe said black magic had been used, and that the problem was getting worse in Brimstone."

Gran nodded thoughtfully. "That is true. We haven't had a murder around here for decades. Brimstone is a quiet, accommodating town. Many beings live happily side by side. As soon as my silly ankle is better, I'll be having a long chat with Blythe. Cassia, how did Blythe know where you were?"

I smiled and lowered my cup. "Sarah, the butterfly, told her."

Gran smiled too. "I'm so glad you found Sarah. How's she doing?"

"Back to full health. And back with the other butterflies. Gran, you should have seen the butterflies on the tree at the end of our path. They were dancing! It was like the whole tree was alive."

"They were singing too," Stanley said.

"Were they?" I asked. "I didn't hear them."

Gran explained, "Our cats have sensitive hearing. It can come in quite useful sometimes. I can't believe Tansy held that poor butterfly captive. I suppose Tansy was worried Sarah would reveal it was her who'd sent the message to Jonathan." Her face wrinkled in concern. "Did you find out who attacked me?"

I nodded. "It was Flint. He's the one who tried to attack me too. He confessed to Anju who then told Blythe. He's in a heap of trouble with everyone."

Gran's face wrinkled even more. "Why would Flint do that? He's never caused any trouble before. I know he's a hothead, but he's never done anything like this. There's definitely something evil in the air."

Stanley tapped his paw on the bedcover. "Cassia, tell Esther what Luca told you when he walked you back home." He let out a little snigger. "Luca had one of his strong arms around Cassia all the way."

"He was just being friendly," I said indignantly. Stanley was turning into a snitch. I'd be having words with him later.

I put my cup down, and said to Gran, "Luca had been to a meeting with some other guardians at Blythe's house. Blythe had been travelling the lands beyond Brimstone as she'd heard rumours of evil acts. She spoke to other witches who said their towns had been affected. Their crime rates were on the increase, and there were more and more incidents of black magic being used. Blythe told the guardians they would need to patrol Brimstone more and be vigilant for any crimes."

Gran shook her head slowly. "This is all very worrying. Does Blythe know where the black magic is coming from?"

"Not yet. She's going to be conferring with the other witches. Also, she's going to interview Tansy and see where she got her supply of black magic from." I sighed. "Gran, I can't believe Tansy forced Jonathan to kill himself. After all he'd been through, he deserved happiness."

Gran patted my hand. "I know, but you found his killer. That will be some comfort to Anju. I'm not sure you went about your investigation the right way by going into Tansy's house like that, but you got there in the end. You and Stanley did a wonderful job." She looked Stanley's way. "This adventure has done wonders for you, Stanley. You don't look as skinny."

I gave him a fond look. Yes, he did look a tad healthier. I suddenly realised I hadn't had one single headache since starting this investigation. And my stomach ulcers hadn't made themselves known at all.

Gran patted my hand again. "Cassia, have you given any thought to this witch business?"

"What do you mean?"

"Have you accepted the fact that you're a witch?"

"I have. I don't think I'm a very good witch. I didn't mean to nearly kill Tansy."

Gran gave me a smile. "You just need to practise more. Cassia, this is a big question, but I have to ask it. Will you work with me in Brimstone investigating crimes? I'm going to have my hands full with this wave of black magic heading our way. It could even be a full-time job."

I looked down at my lap. I didn't know what to say. Was I ready to do this? Was I ready to leave my old life behind?

The doorbell rang which saved me from having to answer Gran's question. I jumped to my feet and declared, "I'll get it."

It was Alastair at the door. He shoved two huge bouquets of flowers towards me along with two big boxes of chocolates.

He held up his hands and said, "Let me speak. Those gifts are for you and your gran. How is she, by the way?"

"She's fine," I said over the top of the flowers.

"Good. Good. Cassia, I need to apologise. I've been such an idiot. I've forced my opinions on you time and time again. I've shown you very little respect, and I'm extremely sorry. I know how lucky I am to have you in my life. You are an amazing person, and I love you so much. I would love to spend the rest of my life with you."

To my horror, he reached into his pocket and pulled out a small box. He opened it and got down on one knee.

Alastair cleared his throat and said, "Cassia Winter, will you marry me?"

I couldn't say anything. I just stared at him.

"Cassia? Did you hear me? I asked you to marry me." He let out a nervous laugh. "Don't leave me hanging here."

My heart softened at the hopeful expression on his face. Despite his faults, I cared for Alastair. He'd always looked out for me.

I knew what my answer was.

Chapter 28

Ten minutes later, I returned to Gran's bedroom. By the look on her face, I guessed she knew who'd been at the door.

I handed Gran one of the boxes of chocolate. "This is from Alastair. There are some flowers downstairs for you too."

"Oh? Was that him at the door?"

Stanley said, "Esther, you know he was. You made Oliver stand at the top of the stairs and listen."

I smiled at Stanley. Him being a snitch could work in my favour. I sat in the chair next to Gran's bed. "Did you hear him propose to me?"

"We did. We didn't hear your reply because you went outside." Gran gave me a searching look. "Can you tell us what your answer was? Or is it private?"

I looked at Oliver and Stanley. They had the same searching looks on their furry faces.

"I told him no."

Stanley leapt to his feet, punched his paw in the air and yelled, "Yes!"

Gran tutted at him. "Stanley, compose yourself. Cassia, are you sure that's what you want?"

"I'm absolutely sure. I'm fond of Alastair, but I don't love him. I don't think I ever have. I ended things between us. He deserves someone who loves him. That life wasn't for me, Gran. You saw how ill I was becoming." I looked Stanley's way. "You saw what it was doing to Stanley. I have to be my true self, and so does Stanley."

Gran reached out and gave my hand a small squeeze. "I think you're making the right decision. Tell me, how did you feel when you used magic?"

I grinned. "I felt awesome. Despite the dangers involved, I'm glad I found Jonathan's killer."

"Do the supernatural beings bother you? There are many species in Brimstone."

"They don't bother me at all. I'd like to know more about them. And if I can help them in any way, then I'd love to do that."

Gran nodded. "I'll let Blythe know. She'll be so pleased. You're going to need a lot of training."

"I know. I'm ready for it." I looked at Stanley. "Well, Stanley, will you be my investigating partner in Brimstone?"

Stanley padded along the bedcover and threw himself into my arms. He leant his head against me and purred. He said, "We're going to make a great team."

I stroked his head. "We certainly are, Stanley."

About the author

I live in a county called Yorkshire, England with my family. This area is known for its paranormal activity and haunted dwellings. I love all things supernatural and think there is more to this life than can be seen with our eyes.

I hope you enjoyed this story. If you did, I'd love it if you could post a small review. Reviews really help authors to sell more books. Thank you!

This story has been checked for errors by myself and my team. If you spot anything we've missed, you can let us know by emailing us at: april@aprilfernsby.com

You can visit my website at: www.aprilfernsby.com

Sign up to my newsletter and I'll let you know how to get a free copy of my new books when I publish them. You can sign up on my website.

Many thanks to Paula for her proofreading work: paulaproofreader.wixsite.com/home

Warm wishes
April

Murder Of A Werewolf

A Brimstone Witch Mystery

(Book 1)

By

April Fernsby

Copyright 2017 by April Fernsby

Book cover: www.coverkicks.com

This is a work of fiction and any resemblance to any person living or dead is purely coincidental.

Printed in Poland
by Amazon Fulfillment
Poland Sp. z o.o., Wrocław